Billionaire FOR HIRE

NEW YORK TIMES & USA TODAY BESTSELLER

CAT JOHNSON

ONE

My running shoes striking the pavement of the path through Liberty State Park kept time with the driving beat of the old Aerosmith song pumping through my wireless ear buds.

Just in case the view of the Hudson River and New York City skyline wasn't enough to entertain me during my morning run, I'd set up my playlist—classic rock—to be timed perfectly to get me from start to finish.

Today I'd reached my apartment building before the final song began. That had me smiling. I'd cut my time, which meant I'd increased my speed.

I was already seeing marked results just a couple of months after I'd decided to kick my fitness routine up a notch—and that had been just one of the changes in my life. I'd also moved out of my Manhattan apartment and to the New Jersey side of the river.

My parents thought I was insane. After all, I was

Brent Hearst, so what the hell was I doing living and working in Jersey?

In their opinion, I was supposed to be paying through the nose for a Manhattan apartment. In my opinion, they were the crazy ones.

The Hudson was just as majestic from the Jersey side and New York City looked far more magical with a little distance blurring out the less savory details.

Most of my old-moneyed classmates from boarding school would probably agree with my parents. Most, but not all of them. Zane Alexander would understand.

He got me. He always had, in spite of our good-natured rivalry, or maybe because of it.

Zane could appreciate how, at times, I hated being a Hearst as much as I loved it . . .

And I couldn't frigging wait for the next time I went running with my good old friend Zane and kicked his ass. Ha! Just let him try to mock me and my lifestyle now. He should run two publishing companies in two different states and see if he had time to work out as much as he did as a SEAL.

I was proud of myself. I'd stuck to my new workout routine in spite of my work and travel schedule. I might not be Navy SEAL material— yet—but by the time I saw him next I should be able to give him a run for his money.

Money. There was an idea. Maybe I should suggest a friendly little wager. Not that I needed the cash, I had plenty of my own, but taking a chunk of Zane's money would give me great pleasure just on principal.

After slowing to a walk to cool down, I finally got to the door of my building. I stopped and pulled out my cell.

I hit pause on the music and checked the time. I wanted confirmation I really had done the run as fast as I thought I had. That's when I saw the text from Zane, the very man I'd been thinking about.

The text was brief and to the point, just like the man himself. He asked me to call him as soon as I could so I punched the screen to return the call while I leaned against the wall and stretched my quad muscles.

When Zane answered, I said, "Well, well, well. Just the man I was hoping to hear from."

"Oh, really. And why is that?" Zane asked.

"I'm going to be in Virginia all this week. I thought we could get together. Go for a run maybe."

I didn't elaborate and tell him I wanted to kick his ass on the running trail to make up for the razzing he'd given me the last time we'd run together. That could be my little surprise.

"Actually, that's why I'm calling. I was hoping you were in Virginia. Any chance you can meet me at my office today?"

"Sure." Though I would rather meet him at a bar than at his office.

Preferably at a place that served food since all this exercise made a man hungry, but I guessed I could grab something along the way.

Or, even better, maybe once I got there I could convince Zane to move our little meeting to someplace near his office. Somewhere that served food with a side of alcohol—or visa versa.

"You free now?" he asked. "I need to run something by you."

Zane never did have any patience for waiting around for anything.

I'd be pissed that he expected me to drop everything to come meet him on a moment's notice if he hadn't done exactly that for me just a couple of months ago when I needed him.

He'd used all his considerable resources and helped me in a big way and I promised if there were anything I could ever do for him, I'd do it. But what he was asking was impossible.

Including the walk to the station and the wait for my train, the trip door to door from my New Jersey apartment to Virginia by rail took the better part of the day.

I laughed. "Sorry. I'm still in Jersey. But I'm leaving in about an hour. I'll be in Virginia this afternoon."

"All right. Text me as soon as you get here."

"Sure. No problem." I rolled my eyes as he continued to make demands on my time.

"Great. Talk to you later." As Zane disconnected it was obvious he hadn't picked up on the sarcasm I thought had been pretty clear in my tone.

With the call done and my plans settled, I yanked open the door of my building, bypassed the elevator and instead ran up the stairs.

I took them with renewed vigor after the break I'd had during the call with Zane and still reached the third floor barely out of breath.

It was nice when even small effort, when done consistently, yielded big results.

While opening the door of my apartment, I decided that might be a good topic for the next company-wide meeting. I hit the face of my smart phone and recorded a note to myself so I didn't forget the idea.

God, I loved technology. But right now, I loved the smart water in the fridge even more.

I grabbed a bottle from the shelf in the door, took a few gulps, and then carried the bottle with me toward the bathroom. I needed to shower and get to the station since apparently I had a meeting later with Zane.

My mental review of my schedule was interrupted as I passed my bedroom on the way to the bathroom. Antonela was there, stripping the bed of its sheets.

I leaned in the doorway. "Hey. I didn't realize you were here."

"I needed to work today instead of tomorrow. Remember? I told you last week." She glanced up from the king-sized mattress she was bent over as I stoically ignored her tempting position.

I could get laid any day—God had blessed me with many attributes ladies liked—but a good housekeeper was hard to find. I wasn't about to ruin our working relationship by tumbling Antonela into that bed she looked so good bent over.

I forced my focus back to the discussion—her working today instead of tomorrow.

"I'm sure you did tell me." And I'd forgotten because of the thousand other things running through my head. If I didn't record a reminder for myself, it inevitably got forgotten. "It's fine. I'm just going to jump in the shower then leave for Virginia."

She straightened up and turned toward me. "I put fresh towels inside for you."

Again I refused to let my gaze stray to where her tight T-shirt hugged her shapely assets. "Thanks. You're the best."

Maybe I'd matured since turning thirty. A couple of years ago I might not have shown such restraint because damn was she hot.

I'd better never go to Croatia because if the women all looked like Antonela, I'd be in big trouble.

Hell, I'd probably come home married even though getting myself a wife—or even a steady girlfriend—was the dead last thing on my agenda. It was right down there next to the second to last thing I'd ever do—sleep with my housekeeper.

I wasn't sure whether to be proud or panicked by my new found mastery over my formerly overactive libido.

I decided not to waste brainpower thinking about it and headed for the shower.

Zane awaited me.

TWO

I'd set up an apartment in Alexandria with all the necessities so all I had to do when I left Jersey was throw my laptop in a bag and I was on my way.

I spent more hours than I'd like on Amtrak, but it wasn't too bad. First Class on the Acela Express was extremely civilized.

Far more civilized than flying or driving. No weather delays. No traffic. I could definitely envision the days of old when society's elite—men like my great grandfather—traveled the country by rail.

I imagined good old William Randolph would be proud that I was keeping up the Hearst tradition, both in publishing and in travel.

There were none of my staff around to interrupt me while I was on board so I was able to get more work done than if I'd been at the office.

Today, I'd put my cell on silent after taking my seat and had handled the bulk of my *To Do* list by the time we crossed into Virginia. Happy, I closed down the laptop, stowed it in my bag and pulled out my phone.

I'd checked my cell sporadically during the trip to make sure there were no emergencies at either office that needed my immediate attention so when I looked now I only had one text. The name on the display had me shaking my head.

Zane Alexander.

Ever impatient, he was obviously checking up on me. The text told me not to forget to call him when I got into town.

I hadn't needed his reminder. I was planning on calling once I was off the train, but I hit to call him back now rather than wait.

"You here?" he asked, without the formality of a hello.

"I am indeed. Just about to get off the train and head over to you."

"Great. What's your ETA?" he asked.

Ignoring that he'd gotten even more demanding since this morning I glanced at the time on my watch and did a quick calculation.

Zane's office was walking distance from the Dupont Circle Metro Station. Since I was already at Alexandria Station, I could easily walk to King Street and hop on the Metro there.

"Give me twenty minutes, give or take," I said.

"Perfect. I'll be here waiting."

Zane, the man in perpetual motion, was waiting? For little old me? Interesting. This must be important. My curiosity was piqued, to say the least.

Figuring I'd know soon enough what this

meeting was about I let it go for now and said, "All right. See you then."

I disconnected and stood as the train came to a stop. Pocketing the cell, I grabbed the strap of my bag and joined the queue of passengers waiting to disembark.

Outside, it had turned out to be a nice day. Warm but not too hot. Sunny here in Virginia after the slightly overcast start to my day in Jersey.

The walk from the Metro felt good after sitting for so many hours. Kicking my annoying friend's ass on the running trail as soon as I could pin Zane down to go would feel even better. I smiled at the thought.

The GAPS office on N Street was small. Just two rooms on the ground floor but it was conveniently located and all that Zane needed for now, I assumed.

And speaking of needs—I was barely in the door when I got an eyeful of Zane's hottie receptionist.

Damn.

Seeing her provided a visceral reminder that I'd been too busy lately to handle some of my own more *personal* needs.

Gorgeous and blonde with mile-long legs more suited for a runway than sitting behind Zane's reception desk, she could fulfill all of a man's fantasies, plus some.

Not a surprise, really. Zane always did have an eye for pretty ladies. He apparently hadn't changed even though he was now a married man. His taste for hot blondes obviously extended to employees as well as wives.

For obvious reasons I would never date any of my own staff—but there was nothing stopping me from dating Zane's employee as far as I could see.

As I walked in she glanced up and smiled. "Good afternoon."

I closed the door behind me and returned her smile.

"Good afternoon, yourself. I'm Brent. Brent Hearst." Hand extended, I strode toward her. "We had the pleasure of bumping into each other here a couple of months ago, but we were never formally introduced."

She stood and walked around the desk and I got a better look at those oh-so-long legs. At a couple of inches over six feet tall, it was rare for me to be eye-to-eye with a woman as I was now with her.

Although closer inspection revealed she wasn't just tall, but also navigating four-inch heels—and doing it as easily as if they were an extension of her own feet.

Walking in *fuck-me pumps* was a female talent for which I had vast appreciation.

"Hi, I'm Chelsea Bridges. Nice to officially meet you, Mr. Hearst." She shook my hand in a strong grasp.

That was another thing I liked on a woman—a nice firm grip. It could be useful for more than just shaking hands.

I knocked that thought from my head as I held on to her hand.

"Call me Brent." When I finally released my hold, I pulled a card out of my breast pocket and handed it to her. "And I do mean that. Call me.

10

Maybe we could go out. For a meal or a drink . . . or whatever else you'd like."

Her blonde brows rose as she took the card. She opened her mouth but didn't have a chance to speak before Zane appeared in the doorway of his office.

She turned her head to glance at her boss, her blonde hair swinging as she did. "Um, Brent Hearst is here to see you."

"Yes, so I see. And please ignore my friend's poor judgment. He obviously doesn't understand what *hands-off my office manager* means." Zane crossed his arms and leaned against the door frame while shooting me a glare.

"Hello, Zane." Shoving my hands in my pockets, I leaned close to Chelsea. "Ignore him. Call me."

Zane was shaking his head as I strode past him and entered his office.

I sprawled in a chair as he closed the door between us and the lovely Chelsea and navigated around his big wooden desk.

"Nice desk." I raised my gaze to meet his.

A desk that large had to be overcompensating for some shortcoming in the man seated behind it. I'd made sure my tone said just that.

He cocked a brow high as he settled in the big leather chair behind his oversized desk and leveled a stare on me. "You really don't know when to quit, do you?"

"Not true. I do know. And I know that time hasn't come yet." I grinned.

He scowled and shook his head. "It doesn't matter. She wouldn't date you anyway."

I rose quickly to his challenge. "How do you

know that?"

"Because she's too smart and independent to fall for your dubious charm."

"Would you like to make a little wager on that?" There was nothing I liked better than a good bet.

"No, I would not."

"Why not? Afraid you'd lose?" I asked.

"No. Because betting on your ability to bed my office manager is just plain wrong."

I huffed out a breath, wondering when Zane had developed morals when it came to betting on women. He'd never had issues with it before. It must be marriage. It had changed him and not for the better.

"You do realize she's way too hot to be hidden away in your office all day. She should be modeling or something.

"She's actually a model as well as an actress. And yet she chose to be hidden away here in my office instead."

It was interesting news, but I wasn't going to give Zane the satisfaction of admitting that. Instead I lifted a shoulder. "Go figure."

He let out a huff of breath. "Anyway, the reason I called," he continued.

"Yes, why did you call?" I asked.

It certainly seemed it wasn't so we could go out and have a good time together. And since he wasn't going to let me have any fun with his receptionist I was really wondering why I'd taken the time to come over here.

"I need your help." There was no more joking in his tone.

Gone was my cocky, smart-ass friend and here instead was Zane the businessman.

Or, more accurately, Zane the deadly serious SEAL.

THREE

I'd seen this side of him when he'd worked a case for me earlier in the year.

That the serious version of Zane was back was intriguing. That he wanted my help, even more so.

"You need my help?" I frowned. "On what?"

I mean I could help him with business advice if he needed it, although his father could do that also.

Then again, those two got along like oil and water. Or more accurately like gasoline and fire.

My attention was redirected when Zane used a remote control to turn on a flat screen television I hadn't noticed hanging on the side wall.

A few taps of Zane's fingers on his computer keyboard and the screensaver showing his corporate logo switched to what looked like a website. Specifically the home page of a charity event.

"You have any connections with anyone at this thing?" Zane asked.

I read the name of the event and the not-for-profit it benefited and neither rang a bell.

"Can I see who's running it?" I asked.

Zane clicked some more and the page showing the names of the event committee and donors appeared. He scrolled down and finally I saw a list of some of the more high profile guests.

It was like a who's who of the rich and famous of the Hamptons. Actors. Designers. Celebrity chefs. Corporate moguls.

"Yeah. I know quite a few."

"Think you could wrangle a ticket?"

"A ticket to this event?" I asked, surprised at the question.

He nodded.

"Probably. And why would I want to do that?" I asked.

It was a ten thousand dollar a head fundraiser. One of those things you attended because you had to, kissed a bunch of cheeks, ate tiny food from silver platters, drank strong drinks if you were lucky, and then left the moment the speeches by the organizers were done.

"Because I asked you to," Zane began. I raised a brow as he continued, "and because you owe me one."

It seemed Zane was going to keep me waiting yet again for information. I had more questions than ever but he was correct, I did owe him.

Apparently it was time to pay up.

"I can make a call and see. But why do you need me to get you a ticket? You've got plenty of connections." I would think Zane having a senator for a father-in-law would open all sorts of closed doors.

"I already called and inquired about tickets. Apparently it's very exclusive and sold out—or so they claim. You think you can make the cut and get in?"

It sounded like a challenge. The bastard knew I couldn't resist a challenge.

"Sure. No problem. But why do you want to attend this thing anyway?"

I stood and pulled my cell out of my pocket, before sitting again. I scrolled to my contact list while Zane watched me.

"The ticket is for you to attend, not me," Zane informed me.

I stopped my scrolling and glanced up, frowning. "Me? Why me?"

"Very good question. Given how exclusive this event is, my muscling my way in would look odd. Your attendance, however, wouldn't raise any suspicions."

Zane was right. The Hearsts had a strong social footprint and plenty of real estate in the Hamptons. And the family, myself included, had a history of philanthropy. My wanting to attend wouldn't raise any questions.

In fact, the only oddity in this whole situation was that someone from my family wasn't already on the guest list or the planning committee.

I nodded my agreement. "Makes sense. That still doesn't tell me why you want me at this event in the first place."

"I'll explain that when you get off the call and have the ticket secured."

"Full of intrigue, I see." How SEAL-like of him. I drew in a breath. "All right. I'll give it a try. And I suppose I'll be footing the bill for this ticket?"

I raised my gaze to his before going back to scrolling through my contact list.

"Relax. GAPS will be covering all your expenses."

More and more interesting, but I could see I wasn't getting any answers from him until I had proven I was worthy. And to do that, I needed an official invite to this purportedly exclusive event.

My path to getting a ticket was clear. I had a standing invitation to stay at my Uncle Bunky's place in Bridgehampton anytime I wanted, but I figured at his advanced age he didn't have any current connections to get me a ticket. My aunt, however, did.

I stopped at the number I'd sought and hit the screen to make the call.

"Hello?"

"Aunt Anne. It's Brent."

"Brent. Good to hear from you. It's been too long since we've seen you."

"It has. I was hoping to correct that and spend some time at Uncle Bunky's soon."

"That's wonderful. You'll have to visit us in Water Mill. We're here at the farm."

Exactly what I wanted to hear. "I'd love that. Um, while I have you on the phone, do you know anything about the charity event in Southampton next weekend?"

"The one being held at the Prentice place?" she asked.

"That's the one. I believe it's to benefit a literacy not-for-profit. I'd love to attend. I need a focus for next year's corporate donations and this charity is a perfect fit. But I heard the event's sold out. They're not letting anyone else in."

"Pfft. We'll see about that. How many tickets did you need?"

She'd reacted exactly as I'd hoped. It seemed no Hearst could resist the lure of a challenge.

"How many tickets do I need? Hmm, let me see." I eyed Zane, looking for an answer. He held up one finger. "Just one should do it. It's work so I won't be bringing a date."

"Smart boy. That way you can network . . . and flirt with all the pretty girls."

"Exactly. You know me so well, Aunt Anne."

"I should. I've known you your whole life. All right. I know the event chair. Let me make a phone call. Is this number the best one to call you back?" she asked.

"It is. I look forward to hearing from you. And thank you."

"My pleasure."

I disconnected the call and raised my gaze to Zane. "Now would you like to explain?"

"Do you have the ticket?" he asked.

"I will in a few minutes."

"Then I'll explain in a few minutes." He leaned back in his chair and steepled his fingers, settling in for the wait, I guessed.

Bastard.

I leaned back and folded my arms. I could wait with the best of them.

"So, where you staying in Virginia nowadays?" Zane asked. "Middleburg or someplace equally snooty. Rubbing elbows with the horse set. Playing polo on weekends."

I guess we were going to make small talk until I either got a ticket or not. And, apparently, he was going to take a few jabs at me and my lifestyle while we did it.

"Nope." I shook my head, not at all sorry to disappoint him by blowing his guess regarding my living arrangements completely out of the water. "I've got an apartment in one of the buildings a couple of blocks from the King Street Metro."

"Really?" His eyes widened. "I'm surprised."

I laughed. "You shouldn't be. At this point in my life, with the amount of hours I work and all the traveling I do, the things I look for in a home have become a bit more practical. Such as being able to drop off my dry cleaning with the concierge on my way out. Besides, what the fuck would I do with a horse?"

He lifted a shoulder. "Beats me. I never understood the appeal myself."

I snorted. "You wouldn't. If I remember correctly you never even had a dog growing up. Do you now?"

"No. I'll get around to it—one day."

I had a feeling that *one day* would be when Zane's new bride Missy popped out the first Alexander baby. Then he'd be trading in his second-floor walk-up for a house with a yard and a picket fence.

My cell rang and interrupted my thoughts about

Zane's future progeny. I glanced at the display and smiled.

"That's her. Get ready to explain yourself." I shot him a warning glare and answered the call. "Hello."

"You'll have one ticket waiting for you at the door under your name at the event. She said you can bring a check that night."

I knew Aunt Anne could do it. Grateful as well as victorious, I said, "I can't thank you enough."

"It was nothing. Seriously. At least one Hearst should be on that guest list, if not more than one. It was their oversight."

"My thoughts exactly, but I do appreciate you making the call. I'll be in touch when I get to Long Island and we'll make plans."

"Perfect. Give our love to your parents and sisters."

"Will do. And please tell my ever elusive cousin Amanda I'll expect to see her there when I visit."

"I certainly will. See you soon."

"Sure thing. Bye." I hit the button and tossed the cell onto the desk between us. "The ticket is secured. Now talk."

Even now he paused, like he was reluctant to bring me into the loop.

Finally, he leaned back in his chair and drew in a breath. "Everything I'm about to tell you can't leave this room. You can't tell your family. You can't breathe a word of it to your latest squeeze. You tell no one. Understood?"

Zane pinned me with his gaze, as if sizing up if he could trust me or not.

"Yes." I waited but he still didn't talk. I shook my head at the fact he didn't trust me. "Zane, do you know how many family secrets I'm carrying around? Not to mention confidential Hearst Corp. business? I sit on the board of directors. Even our meeting minutes are top secret. I can keep your secrets. I promise."

After another pause, more annoying and longer than the first, he nodded. "All right."

He clicked the computer keyboard and then spun his chair to face the television on the wall.

I did the same and saw the image had changed from the event page to a picture of a dark haired, middle-aged man.

"Who's that?" I asked, not recognizing him.

"He is Alexey Mordashov, currently the richest man in Russia." Zane spun in his chair to face me again. "And it would look really bad if someone took a shot at him while he was attending a charity event in the Hamptons next weekend. Which is where you come in."

My eyes widened as I shifted my attention from the screen to Zane. "Me?"

FOUR

With all of Zane's hired muscle and firepower at his disposal, I was his choice of bodyguards for this Russian billionaire?

What the hell?

"Would you like to explain that?" I asked, still recovering from the shock of Zane's statement.

"It's pretty simple. I'm figuring Mordashov getting killed on American soil might cause a bit of an international incident, so we're going to make sure it doesn't happen."

I heard his words, spoken as casually as if we were discussing the weather, but they still didn't make any sense. Particularly the *we*, since I was apparently now part of that *we*.

"Why is that our responsibility? Isn't there the Secret Service to handle important shit such as keeping high profile visiting foreigners alive?"

Zane shook his head. "US and Russian relations are complicated. The White House can't appear as if they're giving preferential treatment to a Russian billionaire attending a party in the Hamptons."

"No, I guess not. So then what about private security? Hell, this is a job for GAPS." From what I knew, Zane and his company's security team could handle this with their eyes closed.

"Exactly. It is a GAPS job. And I'm bringing you in on it."

I shook my head. "I really don't understand. I'm supposed to be this guy's bodyguard instead of you? Why? Just because it's a fancy fundraiser? You own a tuxedo. I'll give you my ticket. You can use my name. No one will care."

"It's not the dress code preventing me from going in. It's Mordashov himself."

As I sat there, open-mouthed, still trying to absorb it all, Zane leaned forward.

"Look, this guy is the son of steel workers. He's a completely self-made man. He fancies himself a man of the people and he doesn't think he needs security."

"But you disagree."

"I do, and so does the client. So we're going to provide him with security without him knowing."

"Why?"

"What do you mean? Why what?"

"Why is his life in danger?" I clarified.

I mean you can't throw a rock in the Hamptons without hitting a billionaire so why was this Russian any different?

"Mordashov has this idea. Some sort of hi-tech online educational ecosystem that would educate a person from kindergarten to after retirement.

Lifetime learning, he calls it."

"How is he going to do that?" I asked, thinking this man's concept sounded interesting.

"I guess it focuses on retraining for different workforce needs at different stages of life . . ." Zane's forehead creased with a frown. "I don't know the specifics. His mission isn't the point."

"What is the point?" I asked, still not getting why I was here or why anyone would want to kill Mordashov.

"That he's already aggressively acquiring the corporations he needs to do it and he's got his eye on more he's planning to scoop up in the US. That and his eighteen and a half billion dollar fortune could make him a target."

"Then if you and your client," whoever the hell this mysterious client was, "are that concerned, just tell this Russian guy he has to have security while he's here whether he thinks he needs it or not."

"Like I already told you, we tried and he refused."

"So what? Tell him that's just too bad. He has to have a bodyguard."

Zane pressed his lips together and shook his head. "It's not that simple. He's only going to be in the country a short time. Literally less than a day. It's just easier to not have him or anyone else know that we're concerned or that we're protecting him. I can cover him from his plane to the event and back again. It's easy enough to have one of my guys replace the driver. But inside the event, an uninvited stranger suddenly showing up with a ticket will stick out. Raise suspicions. You being there won't."

Again, I didn't understand. "But what can I do? I'm not trained."

"You've got two eyes, don't you?"

I rolled those eyes now. "Yes."

"And two ears?"

I was getting more than annoyed with him and his game by the second. "Yes, of course."

"That's all you need. Well that, and the communications device I'll give you. As I said, my guy will be parked right outside the house. This thing goes sideways, he can be inside in seconds. All we need is a set of eyes and ears inside the party. Keep an eye on who he talks to. You see anyone or anything suspicious, anything out of the ordinary, you let us know."

"That's it?" I asked, understandably skeptical.

"That's it." He nodded. "I trust you."

"Do you?"

He cocked his head to one side. "You wouldn't be sitting here if I didn't."

I had my doubts about that, because Zane's whole story reeked of bull shit to me. I might not know some of the things he did as a veteran Navy SEAL, but I knew business. And I had my suspicions about why this mysterious client really wanted eyes on Mordashov.

More likely they were watching to see whom he met with while on US soil, perhaps to determine which corporations where in his crosshairs for future acquisition.

That theory made a hell of a lot more sense than this guy refusing security when his life could be in danger.

I eyed my good old prep school buddy and wondered. Was the client lying to him? Was he lying to me? I might have to resign myself to never knowing the truth.

Still, I figured my best chance to find out what was really going on might be to just go through with it. See things with my own eyes.

Jaw set, I said, "Okay."

"Good. Oh, and I need you to block off an hour or two this week for you and me to go to the gun range."

My eyes popped wide. "The gun—" I cleared my throat as it tightened. "Why?"

I had a bad feeling I knew the answer before Zane said, "I want to make sure you're comfortable with a handgun. And I want you to get used to wearing a leg holster."

A leg holster? Jesus. Maybe I was wrong about this being about business because the corporate takeovers I'd been privy to didn't involve weapons.

My narrowed gaze met Zane's. "How do you know I even have a gun permit?"

"That information wasn't hard to find. Besides, I've known you forever. I know your family has a gun collection and I know you got your permit so you could legally inherit that collection."

"That's the word you seem to be missing the meaning of. It's a *collection*. I don't shoot them. We certainly don't carry them around in leg holsters."

"I happen to know that you do shoot them on occasion. I was there for the skeet shooting competition you set up that summer senior year. Remember?"

Shooting skeet was sport. This, what Zane was suggesting, was—I couldn't even put a name to it. Or maybe I could. It was *crazy*.

I shook the idea of this insanity out of my rattled mind. "It doesn't matter anyway. Half of the collection is in California. And the weapons here on the East Coast are all antiques and locked up at my parents' house."

"I happen to have a weapons room right here in the office. We'll pick you out a nice small pistol to fit beneath your pants leg."

Glancing down I eyed the leg of my pants now. When I'd been fitted for my newest purchase of custom-made suits in Italy, the tailor hadn't taken into account room for a leg holster and gun.

Zane continued, "Luckily for me you're compulsive about keeping your paperwork in order. I know you have a full carry permit valid in New York State."

I didn't even want to ask exactly how Zane knew all that. Was it a matter of public record or was he hacking into the national gun registry? I didn't know but at this point I believed anything was possible.

But maybe having a weapon in the Hamptons with me wouldn't be such a horrible thing, given I'd be alone on the inside guarding this Russian guy who Zane claimed had a target on his back.

I sighed and gave in to the fact that he knew more about this shit than I did. "Okay."

When I glanced up, Zane's smile was visibly victorious. I hated when he looked like that. It meant he'd gotten his way, even though I sure as hell hadn't wanted him to. Not in this case anyway.

Me, spying for GAPS, the company full of Navy SEALS and God only knew who else. It was insane. And I felt completely powerless to do anything about it.

But how could I say no? What if I was wrong about my theory and this guy's life really was in danger. If I backed out and something did happen—

Given the current tense climate of international relations, I could only imagine what would happen if the richest man in Russia was assassinated while in New York.

It could lead to World War III. The scenario was enough to make me think that maybe I should take some of my money and build a bunker.

So fine. I'd do it. I'd do exactly what Zane wanted. Still, I felt like I needed to have some control over this situation. Especially now since I'd be carrying a borrowed gun, making it feel as if my life could be in danger as well as Mordashov's.

I drew in a breath. "I'll do this for you, *but* I want to know who the client is."

Zane shook his head. "No can do."

I scowled even though I'd been expecting him to say that. I scrambled to regain some semblance of control over my own life.

"Fine. But I'm paying for my own damn ticket. And I'll be taking the allowed tax deduction for the charitable contribution."

Zane laughed. "All right. If that'll make you happy, go for it." He stood and moved to a cabinet against one wall. "Now, let's get you set up with communications."

That settled, I felt moderately better, as the little boy who lived inside me and loved his tech toys wondered what sort of Super SEAL, hi-tech communications device I'd be getting.

FIVE

"Brent, you copy? Can you hear me?" Zane's questions came through the minuscule device surprisingly well.

I stuck my finger in my ear canal and adjusted the position of the communicator Zane had given me. "Loud and clear."

Wait. Was it *too* loud? If someone were standing near me, would they be able to hear him too? I wasn't certain and I had no one with me I could ask.

I'd just have to be careful and not get too close to anyone inside the party.

Moving on, I had to get prepared for this assignment. "So what's my code name?" I asked him.

"You don't need a code name."

"That doesn't mean I can't have one," I grumbled.

"Fine. You can have a code name. What do you want it to be?"

I thought for a moment before coming up blank. "I don't know. You have any ideas?"

"No." Zane was not only no fun, he was being no help.

I sighed and glanced around Uncle Bunky's Bridgehampton cottage, looking for inspiration.

I was surrounded by a lifetime of his prized mementos. A handwritten copy of the Hearst family tree. Photos of my great grandfather. And the strangest artifact of all—the sled named Rosebud, an exact replica of the one from the movie *Citizen Kane*.

The place was as interesting as the man himself . . . and that was saying something. He'd been wheelchair-bound for decades but he still loved this ocean front cottage, even though it was modest by Hampton standards.

My gaze remained on the sled and I said, "I'll be Rosebud."

"Rosebud? What the fuck?"

"You know. Orson Welles. *Citizen Kane*. Rosebud."

"You're weird."

"I'm too rich to be weird. If anything, I'm eccentric." I walked to the window and took in the view of the clear blue sky that met the Atlantic Ocean on the horizon.

If Zane thought I was eccentric, he should meet some of the rest of my family. But I had to admit my Uncle Bunky got it right when he chose this spot. It was a hell of a view.

"Whatever, *Rosebud*. Are we done now? This was supposed to be a simple comms test. It should have taken like five seconds."

Maybe in the SEALs it would have. Zane needed to remember whom he was working with here.

I snorted. "Hey, you get what you pay for."

Why was he in such a hurry anyway? We didn't have to rush. The charity event didn't start for an hour.

If everything was running according to the schedule Zane had gone over with me, the Russian's private plane had just touched down. The GAPS guy who'd replaced the regular driver should be meeting him now.

I'd already decided that was going to be Alexey Mordashov's code name tonight—*the Russian*.

His real name was too much of a tongue twister to be using it on the radio. Or rather *the comm* as Zane kept calling the little flesh colored piece of plastic shoved deep in my ear.

"And to answer your question, no, we're not done," I said.

I heard him sigh. "What else?"

"What do I call you?" I asked.

"Base. If you need to call me anything, just call me Base," Zane spat out.

He was probably afraid I'd come up with a name for him too. Though the big bad SEAL should have a kickass code name already from his years in the teams, I would think. They usually did in the movies and on TV.

But if that's what he wanted, Base it would be. I could work with that.

"All right. And where are you, Base?"

"I'm parked. I've got eyes on the location."

"You mean the house where the party's being held?"

"Yes."

Was he crazy? He might know guns and comms, but I knew the Hamptons and the people who lived here, and they were very territorial when it came to their privacy.

"You'd better watch out. They're pretty strict about people parking around there," I warned.

Zane snorted. "Yeah, I know. The rich folks don't want any riff raff enjoying their beach."

"Hey, kill the attitude. The Alexanders aren't exactly middle class, you know," I pointed out.

"Don't remind me. But anyway, I should be fine parked here. I'm in a landscaping truck."

My eyes widened at the information. "That's brilliant."

There were so many lawn guys in these neighborhoods, working sun up to sun down seven days a week to keep up with the demand of the sweeping lawns that needed tending in summer, no one would look twice at the truck.

"Thank you. About time you appreciated my brilliance," he said.

"Don't push it." I could make witty banter all afternoon, but the reality of my impending assignment was beginning to descend upon me.

I felt the gun strapped to my leg.

Would I be able to actually use it if I needed to? Could I really shoot a person?

I turned back toward the room, suddenly dry mouthed, and grabbed the bottle of water I'd left on the table. I swallowed, the tightness in my throat making it difficult.

"Are you armed?" I asked. I needed confirmation I wasn't alone in this thing. Yes, the driver would be right outside, but I didn't know him. I knew Zane.

"Yes," he replied.

"But you don't think we're going to need them though, right? The guns."

"It's just for insurance," he confirmed.

"Okay." I nodded even though he couldn't see the motion and drew in a breath to try to steady my pounding heart.

I was seriously getting nervous. I'd tried to joke my way through this assignment I'd fallen into but this was serious shit. If Zane were telling the truth, I was there to protect a man's life. I was the last line of defense between him and death.

Holy fuck. I wasn't prepared for this.

"Brent."

"Yeah?"

"Get out of your own head before you psych yourself out."

How did he know?

"You sure you want me to do this?" I asked.

"Do what? Attend a party? Mingle? Smile pretty for the pictures and report back to me? Yeah. I'm sure. You can do this."

It sounded so simple when he said it like that. Like it was just another charity event.

I'd attended hundreds of those in my lifetime. One was pretty much just like another, except this time I happened to have a hi-tech communicator in my ear and a freaking gun strapped to my calf.

Not to mention a former member of SEAL Team Six staking out the party from a landscaping truck while another member of his team played chauffeur to a Russian billionaire.

Yup. Tonight was just like any other event.

Sure.

SIX

I left my Land Rover running and slid out of the driver's seat as the valet handed me a claim ticket.

For the first time in my life, I took a good look at the guy about to park my vehicle. I really studied him, wondering if he was who he appeared to be.

Had he too been planted here by some organization?

And what if he had been? Another concern bombarded me. Was he a good guy or a bad guy? Security or spy?

I swept my gaze down his body and wondered if there was a communicator in his ear or a gun hidden somewhere on him.

Since I didn't know if I could actually use the weapon on me in an emergency, my newest theory about the valet was particularly disturbing.

Zane was right. I needed to get out of my own head. My overactive imagination was spitting out ideas faster than editors at a pitch meeting. I was psyching myself out just when I had to remain cool, calm and collected.

The valet was probably exactly who he appeared to be, a fresh-faced kid looking to make some cash over his summer break from college by parking cars in the Hamptons . . . and I needed to start acting like who I actually was—Brent Hearst supporting a good cause while enjoying the beach for the weekend.

It shouldn't be hard.

It shouldn't be, but it was.

I waited for the valet to pull away in my vehicle and crossed the driveway toward the home's entrance.

There was a small, tasteful table set up in front for the volunteers to check people into the party.

I stepped up to the two women and forced a smile I could only hope looked natural.

"Brent Hearst. I was a last minute addition to the guest list. I believe there's a ticket being held here in my name. And I still need to pay." I slid the envelope containing a corporate check out of the inside breast pocket of my navy blue jacket.

Luckily the party wasn't formal, so a tuxedo wasn't required—just a leg holster.

"Welcome, Mr. Hearst. We have your ticket right here." The older of the two women treated me to a smile as she took my payment.

She should be happy to see me. There was ten thousand dollars in that envelope the organization didn't have a minute ago.

"Alexandra, Mr. Hearst's ticket is in the box."

As the younger woman looked for the envelope

with my name on it in the box I took a second look at her. Not because I suspected her as I had the valet, but because she and her fresh faced, girl-next-door good looks was well worth spending some time looking at.

The pretty twenty-something volunteer was almost enough to make me forget my real reason for being here.

Almost . . .

"Mr. Hearst." She held out the ticket she'd located with a brilliant smile.

I forced myself to smile back. "Thank you, Alexandra."

She nodded her acceptance of my thanks as her green gaze met mine. "The silent auction is set up on the front porch if you'd like to take a look."

"Thank you. Anything good I should bid on?" I asked.

No, I wasn't flirting.

Okay, maybe I was flirting a little bit, but the real reason I was stalling was because I knew the Russian's car hadn't arrived yet. I thought it would be better if I were outside when it did. That way he'd go right from the driver's protection to mine—God help us both.

Not that I was planning to do anything to protect him except keep an eye on him and call for backup if anything looked off. But if Zane thought that was enough, I couldn't argue.

"That depends on what interests you," the young brunette said, drawing me away from my racing thoughts and back to a much more pleasant subject—her.

She was all business as she spoke. I didn't know if she was being on her best behavior because of the presence of the older woman seated next to her, or because I wasn't as charming as I thought.

"The week in Aspen looks incredible," the other woman chimed in.

"Thank you. I'll check it out." Running out of things to say, which was unlike me, I glanced over my shoulder, looking for the Russian's arrival.

Where was that damn town car? Zane's man needed to drive faster.

There must be traffic. It wouldn't be a surprise. A sunny summer weekend meant guaranteed traffic on Long Island.

As my mind raced I noticed Alexandra watching me with interest. And not the kind of interest a man wanted from a hot woman. More like she was wondering what I was doing hanging around the check-in table in the driveway when there was no doubt incredible food and drinks being served just yards away.

I scrambled for an excuse.

Leaning lower, I feigned confiding in her as I whispered none too quietly, "I hate attending these things alone."

It wasn't true. I usually knew most of the guests and enjoyed networking with those I didn't know, but she didn't know that.

She lifted one well-shaped dark brow. "It's for a good cause."

I felt the censure. I needed to move on. "Yes. You're right."

I straightened and glanced behind me at the drive

again—and let out a breath of relief as a black sedan pulled up.

Hoping against hope it was the Russian, I held my breath as the driver's door opened and a man much too muscular to look like he sat on his ass behind the wheel all day got out.

That had to be Zane's guy. The driver glanced quickly in my direction then moved to the passenger door, swinging it open.

The man I recognized as the Russian from the pictures Zane had showed me stepped out. The driver slammed the door behind him then got back behind the wheel.

He pulled away, hopefully to park somewhere nearby since he was my backup.

The Russian moved toward the table, and that was my cue to make myself scarce. I wanted to keep an eye on the guy, but I certainly didn't want to talk to him. He might ask me a question I wasn't prepared to answer.

My nerves were about to get the best of me already, without making direct contact with the mark or the target or whatever the hell term I should be using for the Russian. Zane hadn't briefed me on that detail.

I wondered what else we'd forgotten to go over as I glanced back at Alexandra. "Guess I'll be getting inside."

As her focus remained honed in on my face, she said, "Enjoy."

"I'll try." I nodded then moved past her.

I climbed the stairs onto the covered porch and walked around toward the side of the house, following the sound of the party.

The porch overlooked the gardens of the gorgeous home. I remained on the corner. There I'd be able to see the Russian as he followed the path I'd taken, and I could report in to Zane before I was surrounded by guests and had to socialize.

"Base. I'm in," I said softly, hoping Zane would hear.

"Good. Now stop talking to me before someone sees you."

He was right. I would look like a crazy person speaking to no one.

I caught myself touching my ear, afraid the communicator had worked its way out as I walked and become visible. I forced my hand down even as I worried that it might fall out and I'd lose my only connection to Zane.

"Okay," I said, the need to talk to him strong in spite of his warning.

"Go get yourself a drink and calm the fuck down, *Rosebud*." Zane stressed my name, which did sound ridiculous now in the midst of this thing.

"Fuck off," I said.

I heard him laugh but couldn't worry about him more because the Russian was now on the porch as well and heading my way.

A drink sounded good. Not just to calm my nerves but because I'd already spotted the bar and it would be a good place to observe the Russian and the other guests.

No one would question the authenticity of my standing there waiting to get a drink.

As I marveled at how even the most routine,

mundane actions seemed beyond me now that I had a subversive reason for being here, I strode toward the bar.

I had a new appreciation for how Zane had survived all those years in the SEALs, keeping his cool under fire when I couldn't seem to keep mine at a cocktail party.

"Enjoying yourself yet, Mr. Hearst?"

I turned at the question to find Alexandra beside me. "Working on it. And please, call me Brent. Are you off duty for the night?"

"Not quite. I've been sent on an errand."

"Ah." I nodded, wishing I were here to enjoy myself because I would definitely enjoy getting to know the lovely Alexandra under other circumstances.

"And what if I were off duty for the night?" She let the question hang suggestively in the air.

Was she flirting with me?

After her businesslike, almost cold behavior at the check-in desk, that took me off guard. And if she was coming on to me, what the hell did I do about it?

With me playing bodyguard, this was not the time or the place, and I was in no shape to reciprocate anyway. I was lucky to string together two sentences as my nerves threatened to cripple me.

"Brent . . ." Zane's voice, heavy with warning, filled my ear.

Startled, I jumped.

Had she noticed? If she hadn't, she'd certainly noticed that I had yet to reply to her.

"Uh, if you were off duty you'd get to enjoy the party. It's a shame you won't be able to, stuck at that check-in table."

"Yes, it is a shame." Her gaze stayed on me for what seemed like forever. Finally, she said, "I'd better be getting back."

As a small smile bowed her lips she tipped her head in a nod and was gone, leaving me to finally release the breath I hadn't realized I'd been holding.

"Jesus." I'd barely breathed the curse but Zane heard it, of course.

"Boy, have you lost your game," he said.

"Fuck you," I mumbled.

"I told you to stop talking to me."

Was he kidding?

"Then stop talking to me," I hissed and considered pulling the damn communicator out of my ear.

I could always put it back in if I needed it, but it might save my sanity to get Zane out of my head. I had enough stress already without him fucking around with me.

I was still deciding if I should risk his wrath and pursue that idea when my Russian target was joined by a woman too beautiful to be real.

Although that described a lot of people in the Hamptons I still felt like I needed to pass on the information.

I wandered to the edge of the party and faced the ocean. I pretended to be admiring the view so no one would notice me talking to myself. "Zane—I mean Base. Come in."

Zane sighed. "Yes?"

"There's a woman talking to the Russian."

"And?"

"What's strange is I don't recognize her."

"You recognize everyone else there?" he asked, as if that notion was ridiculous.

I turned and glanced around and yeah, I might not know everyone personally, but I recognized every guest in attendance at least by sight. I could open any issue of the local Hampton's publication and see these same people pictured at one event or another.

"As a matter of fact, I do. But there's more. She's way too hot. Like abnormally so."

"So you think she's a honeypot."

"A what?" I asked.

"A hot woman sent to cozy up to a man, get him to let his guard down to get something out of him. Or to do him harm."

I got what Zane was insinuating. That she could be a spy or an assassin. But she could also be a model or a gold digger. I didn't know. Just as I didn't know how the hell my life had shifted so drastically that the word *assassin* was even in my thoughts.

I saw a photographer going from group to group snapping pictures. He stopped in front of the Russian and I got an idea.

"Hang on," I whispered to Zane and then I strode toward the photographer.

When he was done with his picture and had turned away from the Russian and the mystery woman, I stepped up to him and extended my hand. "Hey, there. Brent Hearst."

He juggled the camera to his left hand so he could grasp mine with his right. "Um, hi. Paul Schaeffer. Staff photographer. Dan's Papers."

I nodded. "I figured that's who you worked for. You guys always have the best pictures of the events out here."

"Thank you. I appreciate that. Uh, did you need something? I'd be happy to include you in the spread if that's—"

"Actually I was wondering if you knew who *she* was." I angled my body toward the Russian and his lady companion and tipped my head in that direction.

"Oh." He grinned. "Gotcha. She is an attention-grabber. Hang on. I can tell you exactly." He pulled out a small notebook and referred to his scrawl on the pages. "She's Viktoria Mikhelson."

"Mikhelson." I repeated the name as it rang a bell. The familiarity nagged at me but I couldn't pin down exactly why. Finally, I remembered. "Wait, is her father Leonid Mikhelson?"

"Don't know." The photographer shrugged.

I'd done some research after Zane had given me this more than odd assignment. Mikhelson was on Forbes's list of the world's richest men right along with Mordashov. I couldn't recall how he'd made his money, but I remembered he'd founded some art museum and had named it in honor of his daughter.

So that was the connection. She wasn't an assassin. Just another rich Russian. Two Russian billionaires at one party, it made sense they'd hang out together.

Feeling confident I'd done my due diligence, I

said, "Thank you, Paul. You've been very helpful."

"No problem." The photographer lifted his camera. "Picture?"

I laughed. "Sure, if you really want it. Don't feel obligated."

He shook his head. "Of course, I want it. The Hearsts are a part of Hamptons history."

"I suppose you're right." For better or worse. Not this particular Hearst, but as far as some other members of my family, yes, he was correct. I leaned one hand against the porch post. "Here good?"

"Perfect." He snapped the shot and then said, "Thanks."

"Thank you. I look forward to the article." When he'd moved on, I turned and made my way toward the bar—again. Maybe I'd actually get there this time. But before I did, I whispered, "Base. You get all that?"

"Yeah. Searching her now. I'll send a photo to your cell just to confirm it's really her and not someone sent to replace her."

Jesus, I hadn't even considered that possibility. "Someone could do that?"

"Possibly. If she's a close enough match and they don't know each other personally. Wait for my text."

"Okay." And while I was waiting, I finally stepped up to the bar. "Beer, please."

I took the bottle from the bartender just as the cell in my pocket vibrated. I took a sip before heading back to the edge of the party and checking my phone.

The woman in the photo was a dead ringer for

the woman talking to the Russian.

"That's her," I said softly, the bottle hiding the view of my lips for any guests who might be looking.

"Roger that."

My lips twitched, enjoying that Zane had lapsed into military speak.

I was starting to really get into this mission.

Russian billionaires. Covert communicators. I felt like James Bond, right down to the presence of the mysterious Bond girl. But I'd seen enough of those movies to know that good old 007 tended to get himself into trouble when he succumbed to the charms of the uber-sexy beauty.

She usually tried to kill him, if not during sex, then right after. Observing the scorching hot Russian heiress in front of me, I had to admit that it wouldn't be such a bad way to go.

I glanced back at the porch and remembered there was also the lovely volunteer assistant Alexandra—she'd make a very enticing Moneypenny in my Bond movie scenario.

All right, maybe I was getting into the intrigue a bit too much but with as uneventful as this assignment guarding the Russian had been so far, I didn't see a problem with a little mental distraction.

Speaking of the Russian . . . I swept the area with my gaze and realized I could no longer see him.

Where had he gone?

While I'd been fantasizing about Alexandra, he'd disappeared somewhere. I didn't know where but he was, indeed, gone.

Shit.

"What's wrong?" Zane's question held a good dose of panic and I realized I'd muttered the curse aloud.

I strode toward the house and spotted the Russian and the heiress through the window. A closer look proved they were in deep conversation while studying a painting on the wall of the home.

Art. The heiress's, and her father's, passion.

Phew. Crisis averted.

"Nothing. It's fine. I see him," I told Zane.

Silently I promised myself I'd stop daydreaming even if nothing exciting was happening.

With any luck the rest of the evening would prove to be just as boring. In my current situation, boring was good. I just needed to remember that.

The leg holster starting to chafe my leg should serve as a good reminder. At that thought I took another swallow of the one beer I'd allow myself tonight and wished it were whisky instead.

SEVEN

It was early the next morning when my cell rang.

The name on the display told me it was my GAPS boss, good old Zane.

I answered, "Good morning."

"Are you, uh, alone?" he asked, the word alone heavily laden with innuendo.

I frowned. "Yes. Of course, I'm alone. I was working your job last night. When the hell would I have had time to pick up anyone?"

"You know what I'm asking."

Yeah, I knew what he was asking and I felt the insult to my core. "No, Zane, I didn't spend the night with your target's honey pot from the party, so don't worry."

"She wasn't a honey pot and Mordashov wasn't a target—" Zane sputtered to a stop. "You know, you really need to stop watching so many crime dramas on TV. There's nothing real about them and you sound ridiculous misquoting shit you hear in them."

More insults. Why was I friends with Zane again?

Letting out a huff, I said, "First of all, you taught me the term honey pot, not television. And secondly, if TV is so inaccurate maybe you should do something about it. Be a story consultant or a fact checker or whatever. Have Chelsea hook you up with someone in the biz. She must know people in the industry from her acting gigs."

There was a brief moment of silence. "How do you know Chelsea has industry connections? Please tell me you're not sleeping with her."

I could almost hear the frown on Zane's face.

"You told me she was an actress, dickhead. And no, I'm not sleeping with Chelsea." At this point, all I could do was sigh at the ridiculousness of it all. "You know, Zane, I really wish I got laid half as much as you think I do."

"You get plenty. Don't act like you don't."

It wasn't like I was some sort of man whore. So I liked women and they liked me. So what?

I let out a snort at his accusation. "So did you, not so long ago."

"Ancient history," he said. "I'm very happily married now."

"Fine. I'll concede that point. But I'm not married so I'm free to do what I want and with whom."

"Not with Chelsea or Viktoria, you're not."

"You left out Alexandra from last night. Don't forget her." I scowled at being told what to do.

I'd made it a point not to listen to my father as

often as possible growing up. I sure as hell wasn't going to listen to Zane now.

"Thanks for reminding me. Stay away from Alexandra too."

I drew in a sigh and shook my head as he continued to be ridiculous. "Anyone else off limits? Wait. You know what? Why don't you just email me a list? That way I can keep it on my phone and consult who I'm allowed to date."

"Yeah, yeah, whatever. What's all that noise I hear? Are you out and about already this morning? Or did you never get to bed last night?" Zane asked.

Again I scowled at what sort of opinion he had of me. Like I was some socialite who closed the bars every night then went in search of an after-party. I couldn't run two companies plus keep up with my other responsibilities if I partied until sunrise then slept the day away.

"One day I'm going to take you with me for a typical workday and let you see exactly what I do."

"Sure. And I'll do the same with you for mine. But until then, how about you answer the question?"

"That question being where I am this morning? Not that it's any of your business, but I'm waiting in line to get coffee."

"Where are you? Starbucks?"

"Pfft. No. Way better than Starbucks. Montauk Bake Shop."

Zane laughed. "You drove all the way out to Montauk for coffee? I hope it's worth it."

"It is, but I'm not here for the coffee. I'm here for the jelly croissants. They're legendary and they

51

sell out so you have to get here early. Especially in season."

"These jelly things must be good to get you up and out this early."

"They are. Believe me." And I hated to tell him the croissants were going to take precedence over his call any minute now.

The moment the line crept up far enough that I was no longer outside on the sidewalk, but actually inside the bake shop, this call was over. I didn't understand the shop's no cell phones rule, but I wasn't going to question it or break it. Not when my annual fix of jelly croissants hung in the balance.

"You still here in New York?" I asked, feeling generous. "I'll grab an extra one for you."

"Thanks, but I'm back in Virginia. I left as soon as Mordashov's plane took off last night."

So the Russian was gone and, consequently, so was Zane.

I guess his life did move as fast as mine. Or faster, since I was currently planning on spending a lazy Sunday gorging on jelly croissants and then lunching with the family in the Hamptons before heading back to Jersey.

Reviewing my agenda for the day, maybe I did understand Zane's razzing me sometimes. But I didn't deserve all of it because I did work hard—when I worked.

Work hard. Play hard. Nothing wrong with that.

"So that's it then. My assignment is over?" I asked.

"That's it," Zane answered.

"Oh." I'd never wanted it in the first place, but

now that it was finished, I felt a little let down.

He laughed. "Don't sound so disappointed. It was a success. Mordashov left New York as healthy and happy as he arrived."

"Is he still in the country? How do you know he's safe wherever he is now?" My portion of this job might be over, but I wouldn't feel a sense of completion if I didn't see it through all the way to the end—even if it was from afar while getting coffee and pastries.

"Remember, it was my guy driving his town car. So we had eyes on him from the Hamptons right up until he took off from JFK for Heathrow. He's heading to London next so he's now their problem. Not ours."

"That's very good to hear."

"Anyway, thank you for your help. You're done. I'll grab the gun and the comm from you next time you're in town."

The gun and holster I'd be happy to return, but I frowned at the idea of turning in my communicator. "I don't get to keep the comm?"

Zane laughed. "No. All equipment gets checked back in after an op so we have it for the next one. What in the world would you do with it anyway? You won't be able to use it. It only works with our system."

I might never need it again, but I was still unhappy that he wanted it back. I kicked at the crack in the sidewalk outside the bakery. "Who knows? Maybe I'll have to help you again."

"I'm pretty sure this is going to be a one shot deal. No worries, Brent. Your debt to me has been paid in full. I appreciate your help. You're done."

I didn't like losing all my James Bond paraphernalia, but I said, "All right."

"Hey. You in line or what?" The cranky complaint came from a gravelly-voiced old man behind me.

Apparently I wasn't up the butt of the customer in front of me closely enough for the impatient guy behind me.

"Yeah, I'm in line." I turned away from him. "Zane, I gotta go."

"All right, Rosebud. Enjoy your jelly donuts."

Regretting my choice of code names, which would no doubt haunt me for years, I scowled.

"Jelly croissant and you don't know what you're missing." I disconnected the call without the courtesy of a goodbye.

I pocketed my cell before I incurred the wrath of the counter help, then stepped through the doorway and into the shop that did an insanely large amount of business in a crazy small number of square feet.

Once it was my turn, I was in and out fast. The staff always was efficient. They had to be given the number of customers waiting.

I'd justified ordering a dozen jelly croissants because I was stopping by Aunt Anne's today.

The reality was, I'd probably end up eating more than my share. I wasn't out here half as much as I used to be as a kid. Work and adulthood got in the way.

I'd run off the calories anyway.

With the box of pastries in one hand and my coffee in the other, I pushed through the door and headed down the sidewalk—and walked directly into someone who had me smiling.

I stopped in front of her. "Alexandra?"

"Good morning, Mr. Hearst. And you can call me Alex. Now that I'm *off duty* we don't have to be so formal." Her smile was warmer today. More genuine now that Alex was off-duty.

Alex. The name fit her. Especially now as she was dressed in yoga pants, sneakers and a T-shirt with her hair pulled back in a ponytail.

"Alex, it is. But only if you call me Brent." I smiled.

The corners of her lips twitched up. "Okay. I'll give it a try."

"Good." Her answer as much as the good-natured humor with which it was delivered made me happy. "Funny seeing you again so soon. What a coincidence, huh?"

She lifted her shoulders in a shrug. "Not really. Who could be this close and not make the trip to get a jelly croissant at the bake shop?"

My eyes widened at her comment. "A woman after my own heart." I held up the box. "That's exactly what I came here for."

"A whole box." She bobbed her head. "A true fan. I'm impressed. I was going to indulge in just one. Now you've gone and upped the stakes."

A man clad in a white apron leaned outside and slapped a sign onto the glass door of the shop. "Jelly sticks are sold out, folks. Sorry."

"No." Alex's smooth forehead furrowed in a frown. She let out a loud sigh. "I knew I should have gotten here earlier."

The guilt struck me hard. If I hadn't bought a full dozen, the people in line behind me—Alex included—could have gotten some.

"Come with me." I tipped my head toward a vacant park bench.

She followed me as I put the box down on the bench and broke the tape that held it shut.

"Sit." I used a napkin to pick up one delicate tempting confection and held it out toward her as she sat. "Here."

Alex shook her head. "No. I couldn't take—"

"Of course, you can. I bought a dozen. Honestly, you'll be saving me from my own gluttony."

Her gaze moved from the croissant to my face. "If you're sure . . ."

"I'm sure." I handed it to her and went back to get one for myself.

Flipping the lid shut, I settled in the sunny spot on the bench next to her and leaned in for my first bite.

Since I'd given her my napkin, I had none for myself. I knew from experience that jelly was going to squirt out the end of the croissant and make a mess, if not on my pants, then at least on the sidewalk, but I didn't care. It had been too long since I'd indulged in this particular treat.

I groaned as the flaky, buttery croissant melded with the smooth sweet jelly.

A giggle next to me brought my attention around to Alex as she watched me eat and laughed.

I noticed she'd been a bit more delicate than I had. She'd managed to keep her jelly and crumbs contained in the napkin while mine splattered the pavement.

"Don't mock a man in ecstasy," I warned.

"I'm not. It's just nice to find someone who appreciates a Montauk institution as much as I do. I'm afraid that not one of those women at the party last night would even come near this thing."

"Their loss." I'd choose a woman I could dive into a box of pastries with over one who tried to survive on black coffee any day of the week.

She took another bite and shot a squirt of red jelly onto her hand, which she quickly licked off before her gaze cut to me and her cheeks flushed. "That was completely crude of me. I'm sorry."

I laughed. "Don't worry about it. You can lick jelly in front of me any time."

"Thank you. You as well." She licked her fingers one more time as I enjoyed the sight.

"I will. Thanks." I grinned and reached for my coffee cup, which I'd set on the ground when I'd abandoned it in favor of the croissant. "Nothing like Montauk Bake Shop's hot coffee and jelly croissants."

"I would normally agree but I'm not sure it's worth that line just for the coffee. But I'm a happy girl with the croissant. Thank you."

I noticed Alex had carried a stainless steel travel coffee mug with her.

"Bring that cup over here." I pulled the plastic top off my own paper to-go cup.

"Oh, no. I couldn't take your croissant and your coffee too."

"Come on. There's plenty to share. I got a large." And that was another reason I loved this place. A freaking large coffee was exactly that—a large coffee and I didn't have to speak in another language just to order it.

She tipped her head to one side, eyeing the liquid in my cup. "Cream and sugar in there?" she asked.

"Yup. Both. And plenty of it." I waited.

Was she an artificial sweetener and skim milk girl or could we share coffee with all the good old-fashioned decadent additions?

"Thank God. If you drank it with no sugar, I would have had to say no." She popped the top off her reusable cup and thrust it forward. "I'd love some.

I gladly filled it. She'd passed the coffee test with flying colors. I wondered what else we had in common.

She drew in a long sip and groaned. "That's good. Thank you so much."

"You're most welcome." Small talk over pastries and coffee with Alex might be the best date I'd been on in a while, even if this wasn't by any stretch of the imagination a date. I decided to extend our interlude and start a conversation that had to do with more than our food. "So, what did you think of last night's party?"

"I think it was a success. The organization brought in a lot of donations."

I laughed. "Okay, now take off your organizer's hat and answer again. Did you enjoy it? Did you speak with anyone interesting?"

"Besides you, you mean?" She smiled.

"Besides me." Though I liked how she was thinking.

"It was definitely an interesting mix of people. More so than usual thanks to the Russian component in attendance."

I raised my gaze and found her watching me.

What should I say? If I were a normal guest, I shouldn't know even half as much about the Russians as I did.

"You're right." I nodded. "It was an interesting mix of people."

There. That reply was generic enough it shouldn't tip my hand.

She cocked a brow high. "It's okay. You can be honest."

I nearly choked. I cut my gaze to her. "Honest about what?"

"I saw you watching them. I understand. She's not only gorgeous, she's a freaking heiress. Hell, I was staring at her too."

Relief hit me. She wasn't talking about my Russian at all. She was referring to the other Russian. Viktoria.

Calmer now that we weren't in dangerous territory where I might spill some of Zane's secrets about Mordashov, I relaxed.

"Eh, I guess she's okay, if gorgeous and rich are your type, that is." I grinned, teasing.

"Isn't gorgeous and rich everyone's type?" she asked.

I lifted one shoulder. "I don't know. I have more of an affinity for women with jelly on their face."

Her eyes widened as she covered her mouth with her hand. "Do I?"

Smiling, I reached out. "Here. Let me."

She lowered her hand and I brushed a thumb over the faint red smear. It didn't come off and I did probably the worst thing one person could do to another, especially someone they barely knew. I licked my thumb then rubbed off the stain.

Okay, yeah, that felt way too intimate. I leaned back. "Got it."

Pink cheeked, she said, "Thanks."

"Anytime." I cleared my throat. "So, you heading out today? Unless you live out here—in which case, I'm jealous."

She laughed. "I don't live out here, unfortunately. I'm heading back to the city in a bit. It's been a nice weekend at the beach but it's time for Cinderella to get back to reality."

"I'm heading back today too."

"Manhattan?" she asked.

"Jersey City, actually. But I've got the best view of Manhattan you've ever seen from my apartment."

"Nice." She nodded. "You know, if you're interested, there's another charity event next weekend. It's at the New York Center for Independent Publishing on 44th Street. Gorgeous old building. Beautiful architecture. The event is a reading by Billy Collins. He's hysterical."

I nodded. "He is. I've seen him perform. Years ago. What day is this event?"

"Friday night. Eight o'clock performance followed by a reception."

"Sounds interesting. Are there tickets still available, do you know?" I asked, more interested in the fact that she'd be there than Billy Collins.

"I think I'll be able to squeeze you in." She leaned in conspiratorially. "I know the marketing director of the not-for-profit."

Her smile and joke had me guessing, "Would that be you, perchance?"

"Sadly no. I'm just a volunteer."

"Never say just a volunteer. It's the most important job title a person can hold."

"Thank you."

"You're welcome. And as for the event, it's a date."

She reacted to the word date. I watched her expression morph from surprise to what I'd like to think was satisfaction.

She smiled. "It's a date."

Now all I had to do was keep my date with Alex on the down low so I didn't get a lecture from Zane since she was on my No Date List from him.

That made going out with her even more enticing.

Zane should have known better. Breaking the rules was the only thing I liked better than rising to a challenge.

Silly man.

EIGHT

Since she needed to contact me regarding the event, Alex now had my digits and I had hers.

Looking down at my cell phone, at the contact listing I'd created after she'd typed in her number, I smiled and hit to open a new message window.

How about I pick you up for the event?

I took it as a good sign when the bubbles immediately appeared in the text box telling me she was typing back. I had no patience for waiting when I was excited about something, so I was more than happy when her response came back right away.

In Queens?! Thanks but that's crazy. I'll meet you there.

To say I was disappointed was an understatement. Her elusiveness made me want to pick her up even more.

I'm fine with crazy. I'll pick you up.

I sent her my reply, realizing that being in a relationship with a woman in Queens while I lived in Jersey was going to add a logistical challenge, but again, I loved a good challenge.

In a relationship. That train of thought made me pause.

What did I want from this thing with Alex?

I thought about it and about her. I could see us together even though I knew next to nothing about her. Not even her last name.

That had put a damper on any cyber research since I couldn't even look her up on Instagram if I didn't have her last name.

I'd already been through the Hamptons event website and hadn't found her name on any list of guests or staff.

That did seem a bit odd since I would have thought they'd at least list the names of all the volunteers, but no Alexandra.

Since Zane's assignment had given me a healthy dose of doubt and paranoia about who people were and were not at that event, I might have been suspicious of Alex after not seeing her name listed *if* I hadn't seen her there, seated at the check-in table next to one of the event organizers.

She'd had her hands all over the tickets and the donor checks. They must trust her, so I should be able to trust her as well. If she were pretending to be someone she wasn't, the organization was in more peril then I was.

I quickly dismissed any remaining shadow of suspicion and returned to my dilemma—getting to know more about my lovely escort for the evening. I couldn't learn more about her online, so I'd have to do it the old fashioned way—in person on our date.

I liked this girl. I didn't know if she was rich or poor, gainfully employed or not, and I didn't care.

That I felt the strongest connection with her while we'd both been covered with jelly proved there was something there between us. Chemistry. Fate. Coincidence. Serendipity.

I didn't know what. All I knew was that any woman who knew about the hidden gem that was Montauk Bake Shop, and appreciated it as much as I did, was a person worth getting to know better.

I'd been more interested in my conversation with Alex sitting on the bench on the sidewalk than I had with any of the party chatter.

She was the only person I'd really enjoyed speaking with while at an event teeming with the elite of the Hamptons charity party circuit.

Beauties and billionaires, both international and domestic, had been at that event and not one of them had inspired me to want to see them again except for Alex.

Even the visit to my family on my way home had shown me I was too far removed from the world of high society now to enjoy it for long.

Eyeball deep in my publishing companies, with a bit of Zane's intrigue thrown in, I had next to nothing in common to discuss with my family who was completely wrapped up in Hamptons society. Our lives revolved around completely different things.

I was interested in speculating about Jeff Bezos's next acquisition, while they were wondering who was selling or buying which properties. I was waiting for the next industry-changing announcement from Amazon and what it would mean to the state of publishing, and they were chatting about who'd gotten divorced recently.

It was painfully obvious that trying to be a working-class Hearst, as well as a Hearst trust-fund heir, was a two-sided coin and I was going to have to become adept at balancing both worlds.

I had a suspicion regarding which world Alex belonged to, even without knowing her last name or anything more about her, and that was fine with me.

Preferred actually.

If I was going to start a relationship, I wanted it to be grounded in the real world. I might still end up fodder for gossip, unavoidable given my last name, but I could deal with it with the right woman by my side.

I leaned back in my chair and realized I'd been making a lot of assumptions here. Alex might not be interested in anything more than getting me and my money to this next fundraiser. But somehow I didn't think that was true.

I'd find out either way soon enough. Tonight, probably.

I heard the text alert and glanced down.

Stop! I'll meet you inside the front door at 7:30. I have your ticket.

She still wasn't going to let me drive her to the event.

Maybe there was something wrong with me that I always had to have my way. Perhaps my privileged upbringing was to blame. Whatever the case, I couldn't let this thing go.

Leaning forward, I searched online for directions to the venue. Then expanded the map that came up in the search results to include bars and restaurants nearby.

If I couldn't convince her to let me pick her up, the least I could do was buy her dinner.

I grabbed my cell and punched in another text.

How about we meet for dinner before the show?

The bubbles appeared again, right after I sent the text, just as I new they would.

You are persistent, aren't you?

I smiled and typed in my reply.

It's my best quality.

As expected, her reply was quick and sharp.

Not sure I agree but okay. When and where?

Victorious, I typed in the name and address of the restaurant I'd found online and a time.

She responded with a short but encouraging *K* and that was that. Dinner and a show—okay, a fundraising event that included a reading. Close enough to a show to make me believe this was definitely an official date.

Finally satisfied with the plans for the evening, I secured reservations for us, then got back to work. I had a long list of things to get through today and with the date with Alex on the horizon, no way was I working late tonight.

NINE

If I had any doubt about classifying tonight as a date, it was erased the moment Alex walked into the restaurant.

A woman didn't look that good for just any old charity event. This was definitely date attire.

Her red dress had every eye in the place turned toward her when she walked through the door, mine included.

I'd arrived early and was waiting at the bar.

The color caught my attention but it was the woman who held it. The fabric clung to her every curve, but it was the whole package rather than the dress itself that made her irresistible.

My gaze swept down her body, from the swell of her breasts above the plunging neckline, all the way down to the red high heels that gave me all sorts of inappropriate ideas. Maybe I was a sexist pig but I couldn't help myself.

Swallowing hard I forced my focus back up to

her face and man, she was gorgeous.

She'd been pretty before, but tonight, with her hair swept up to expose the bare skin of her neck and shoulders, and makeup that made her eyes stand out like beacons beckoning me to move closer, she was breathtaking.

I'd had the pleasure of spotting her before she saw me so I could fully appreciate her unobserved.

When I finally got my head on straight, I stood and moved toward her just as she noticed me and smiled.

That smile brought my attention to her lush lips. I had to fight the urge to kiss them as I leaned in and brushed a chaste kiss to each of her cheeks.

"Hey. You look great." That I managed to sound smooth even as I was lusting after her was a testament to the sheer number of dates I'd been on in my life. Pleasantries were second nature at this point.

"Thank you." The sexy as sin woman before me managed to look shy, almost embarrassed at the compliment as her gaze dropped away from mine. She finally brought her eyes back up. "So do you."

I liked the glimpse of the uncertain girl I'd gotten to know on that bench over jelly croissants.

"This old thing?" I smiled and frowned down at the suit I'd had custom made in Milan last time I was there. It cost more than I used to pay in rent on my Manhattan apartment before I moved—and that was no small sum.

She rolled her eyes at my corny joke, and I didn't blame her one bit.

"The table will be ready in a few minutes. What

can I get you to drink?" I set my hand on her elbow to steer her toward the spot where I'd left my drink on the bar.

"Um. I'm not sure." She hesitated. "A glass of white wine maybe?"

"White wine, it is." I flagged down the server and ordered as she slid onto a barstool and laid her small purse on the bar.

Her gaze quickly swept the space, taking in everything. The bar patrons. The staff. The diners in the adjoining space. Even the back exit.

When her gaze finally landed again on me, she smiled and broke eye contact once more, looking shy that I'd been watching her.

I found the dichotomy within her intriguing. Not just tonight but since I'd first met her at the Hamptons fundraiser.

I remembered how she'd been organized and efficient, juggling the uber-rich and their money at the check in desk all while keeping the event chairs happy.

And tonight she was all cool sophistication in dress and appearance, head held high as she strutted through the front door and spoke with the hostess . . . until she saw me.

Then, through the cracks, slipped out the shy, indecisive part of her. She'd gone from a sharp smart woman to one who grew uncomfortable at receiving a compliment and couldn't decide if she wanted a drink or not.

Was it me? Did I make her nervous? And if so, why?

Maybe it was because she liked me. I enjoyed

that idea—probably too much. Not because I wanted to make Alex uncomfortable, but because I loved the idea that she might be attracted to me.

The way she looked tonight, combined with the way I felt—we'd be combustible if she wanted me even half as much as I wanted her.

The server delivered the wine and Alex reached out and took one tentative sip. She caught me staring at her and put down the glass, fidgeting on her stool.

Shit. I needed to take it down a notch. She was the first woman I'd been interested in—I mean really interested in—in a long time. The last thing I wanted to do was send her running.

If it meant I had to tone down my usual level of first date charm, I would.

I sipped at my beer—a local craft brew—and considered how to play this. Cool indifference? Professional?

Fuck it. I couldn't help myself. I said, "You really do look beautiful tonight."

"Thank you."

As expected, the compliment meant I'd sacrificed eye contact with her as her focus skittered away again.

Time to bring her back to me . . . I changed the subject to something she'd be more comfortable with.

"Thanks for telling me about the event. And I did a little research on the history of the venue. It was really interesting."

"It is." She nodded.

I nearly rolled my eyes at my own comment. My

conversation was all over the place. My mood too, as I waffled.

One moment I felt the need to coddle her. The next, I had to fight the urge to grab her and kiss her until that shy insecurity disappeared.

There was a middle ground in there somewhere and I became determined to find it.

"I'm glad we got a chance to meet before the show," I continued, in my effort to get Alex to relax.

"Why is that?" she asked.

"Because now we'll have a chance to talk. Get to know each other better."

"Oh?" One shapely brow rose. "And what would you like to know?"

"Well, for starters, I don't even know your last name."

"Having trouble stalking me on Facebook with only my first name?" Now her stare met and held mine, no hesitation.

"Actually, I was going to try Instagram, but yeah." I smiled, not at all embarrassed I wanted to learn more about her. "Sorry."

Not really.

Her lips twitched. "It's okay. I forgive you. There's all sorts of stuff online about you."

"You looked me up." I laughed, loving she'd been thinking about me and cared enough she'd taken the time to stalk me online. "So, anything shocking?"

"No. Not at all." She cocked her head to one side, almost as if that lack of discovery perplexed her.

"Is that a bad thing?" I asked.

"Not bad. Just odd."

"Odd how?"

"It seems like there'd be at least one scandal in your past."

"Oh, there's plenty of scandal. Luckily for me, it's the other members of the large and ever growing Hearst clan monopolizing the headlines."

"But not you?"

"Maybe long ago in my youth I might have been scandal worthy, but remember, back in those days Facebook was just a fledgling site. Social media was nothing like what it is today. It was easy to stay off the public radar."

"And what about now?" she asked while trailing one finger up and down the stem of her wine glass in a way that had my gaze fixed to the motion.

I cleared the lust from my throat and answered, "These days I work so many hours it'd be hard to get into any news-worthy trouble."

She nodded, but something hidden in the depth of her eyes hinted that she wasn't quite buying my story.

Sadly, everything I'd told her was the absolute truth.

"Mr. Hearst?"

The summons brought my attention around to the hostess. "Yes?"

"Your table is ready."

"Wonderful." I looked to Alex and reached out one hand, palm up. "Shall we?"

With no hesitation, she met my gaze, took my hand and said, "We shall."

Coming full circle, the strong confident woman was back and I became even more determined that I was going to get to know all the many parts of this woman. And wouldn't that be fun.

I couldn't wait.

TEN

The evening went well, if I did say so myself.

The dinner conversation flowed easier than I anticipated. Once at the event, the reading was entertaining, as was the reception after the show.

I couldn't have asked for more.

Well, maybe a little more as I pushed open the door to the street.

Alex smiled and thanked me as she walked through but I was far from ready for the night to end.

I didn't care that I had planned to be on the early train to Virginia in the morning. I didn't care that my bed was across the bridge in Jersey and Alex's even farther away in Queens. I didn't want to say goodbye. Especially since we had yet to make plans for when or if we'd see each other again. And even more because I hadn't yet tasted those lips that had taunted me all night.

Outside, she paused on the sidewalk. Finally she

said, "So there's this thing at the MoMA tomorrow evening if you're free. I already have two tickets so it'd be my treat. I don't want you to think I'm only after your donor dollars." She smiled.

"The thought never crossed my mind." Okay, it had, but I wrote that off to temporary insanity resulting from my assignment for Zane.

My plans to head to Virginia in the morning could wait until Sunday. Hell, if I was lucky enough to be able to spend the whole weekend with Alex—and if I got *lucky* in the other sense of the word—I'd gladly take the early train Monday morning rather than give up time with her this weekend.

Ignoring the fact I already had us spending not only Saturday night together, but also all day Sunday too, I said, "I'd love to go. Thank you."

"Good. It should be an interesting event. The Russian will be there too."

Her mention of the Russian grabbed my attention. I'm sure she noticed my surprise as she watched me close.

I scrambled to cover. "Oh? Well, I guess we all tend to run in the same charity circles." I shrugged to add to my illusion of nonchalance, as my mind spun.

I'd have to text Zane this information as soon as possible. He needed to know that Mordashov was going to be back in town.

"I guess that's true," she said. "And it really isn't a surprise since art is Viktoria's field. There's no way she'd miss an event at the museum while she's in town."

"Viktoria." Of course. I nearly slapped myself in

the forehead at that revelation. I rushed to cover my surprise that we'd been speaking about two different Russians. "Yes. I read that she and her father are very involved in the art world."

"It's not every woman who has a museum named after her." Alex continued to watch me with an intensity that belied the casual nature of the conversation.

"No, they don't." I nodded. And I probably should have pretended I didn't know that fact, since I'd discovered it when I'd researched Russian billionaires right before the Hamptons event. Time to change the subject before I revealed too much. "So, did you drive in?" I asked.

"No, I took mass transit."

Excellent. That left me with the opportunity to offer her a ride home. "Then I'm driving you home."

"You don't have to—" she began.

"Alex, I swear—if you think I'm going to let you get back to Queens on your own at this time of night dressed like that, you're crazy or you think I am. I'm driving you home." My tone left no room for debate.

What I said was true. Even if I hadn't been hoping for an invitation inside when I dropped her off, I would have insisted on driving her home.

Her taking mass transit in the daylight during the commuter rush was one thing. But this late on a Friday night was another.

I was about to steer her toward where I'd parked my car whether she liked it or not when she said, "Actually, I'd love to see your view."

After a second of shock, I finally found the capability to speak. "Did you want to come back to my place?"

"I'd love to." The shy version of Alex was obviously gone for the moment. I couldn't say I was sad about that.

I had yet to recover from that *holy shit* moment when she grabbed my hand. "Where's your car parked?"

If my pounding pulse would direct some blood to my brain instead of sending it elsewhere I probably could have answered that question easily.

I forced myself to focus. Glancing up at the street sign, I got my bearings and remembered hours before, when I'd parked in the first spot I saw, excited to get to the restaurant and meet her for dinner.

That seemed like an eternity ago. How things had changed since then.

I found the Land Rover easily enough once I put my mind to it. Soon, we were seated in the vehicle as my mind pinged from one random thought to the next, like a ball in an old arcade machine. It was proof of how Alex's request had thrown me.

Women threw themselves at me all the time. I was used to that. I expected it. But I didn't expect it from her.

It seemed out of character for Alex. But then again, I didn't know her well enough to determine that.

I sure as hell wasn't going to complain or question that this attractive, interesting woman who I craved to distraction wanted to come home with me.

Only a fool would do that and I'd never considered myself a fool.

Maybe the connection I felt was as real and as strong for her as it was for me.

Connection.

Jesus. I couldn't believe I'd even thought that word. It was the kind of thing you heard thrown around too often in romantic comedies or on *The Bachelor*. It never failed to make me roll my eyes.

Not this time.

But this emotional shit didn't happen in real life—at least it didn't happen to me. Yet here I was, hurtling through the Holland Tunnel as fast as the traffic would allow to get Alex back to my apartment.

And not just for sex either, though that was certainly a strong motivation. I was ready for the works with her. Breakfast in the morning. The trip to the museum tomorrow afternoon. Maybe brunch on Sunday after a Saturday night spent once again in my bed. Then maybe a walk along the river if the weather was nice . . .

Shit. I'd be shopping for a bigger apartment any day now if my feelings for her continued to grow at the speed they had so far.

"What's this?"

It was hard enough paying attention to the road with Alex seated in my passenger seat. But her question refocused all of the meager attention I'd managed to keep on my driving dangerously to her.

Once I saw what she held between her fingers I was really in danger of crashing.

It was my fucking comm unit.

I forced my gaze back to the road. "Where did you find that?"

"In the cup holder. What is it?"

Shit. The memory of pulling it out of my ear and tossing it into the console after the party hit me. "Uh, just a blue tooth earpiece."

"It doesn't look like any one I've ever seen before."

"It's a, uh, prototype. You know, Hearst Corp. gets all sorts of products consumers don't see until years later, if at all."

"Oh. Must be nice."

"It can be. I have to return that one though." I held out my hand, feeling the need to get it away from her.

She put the tiny unit in my palm as she said, "That's not so nice if you have to give the gifts back."

"Only some of the more experimental stuff." I slipped the unit into my pocket, far away from Alex's grabby hands.

I'd have to remember to take it with me when I left for Virginia anyway, so it seemed safest there in my pocket.

"And what was experimental about it? Did it do something cool?" she asked, probing deeper into a subject I'd rather she dropped.

I'd dug my hole full of lies so deep I wasn't sure how to get out of it. I should have said it was my uncle's hearing aid since it looked more like that than a cell phone ear bud.

Too late now.

"It uh, has a really long battery life. That was supposed to be the big selling point. There's also the clarity."

"Really? Can I hear?"

"Uh, no. Sorry. The battery's dead."

"So much for that battery life, huh," she said as I felt her gaze remain focused on me.

"Yup. Which is probably why they want it back. So they can improve it." *Shit. Shit. Shit.* I needed to redirect this conversation. "So, tell me more about this MoMA event. What's the dress code?"

"Planning your outfit already?" she asked.

"Always. Gotta look good for the reporters. We could end up on Page Six."

"Just one of the demands of being you, I suppose." There was an edge to her voice that was unsettling.

I'd started out this trip so excited. So hopeful. Yet somehow the comm conversation had derailed our night.

"So, formal? Casual? Business attire?" I asked, bringing us back to the dress code for the event.

"A suit will be fine."

"Suits I've got plenty of." Off-the-cuff answers to unexpected questions, not so much.

I could only hope we'd have moved on from this little bump in the conversation by the time I reached my exit.

If not, I supposed I'd be turning around and driving Alex back home to Queens.

I felt the weight of her hand on my thigh and glanced over.

She smiled and squeezed my leg. In yet another

reversal, the atmosphere between us changed yet again. She moved her hand farther up my thigh and left it there.

I felt the warmth of her touch radiate through the fabric of my pants, so close to where I'd fantasized about her hand—and her mouth—being.

Maybe I wouldn't be driving to Queens tonight after all.

ELEVEN

I'd just opened the door when Alex strode through the doorway and into my apartment.

She turned on the lights before I even got my key out of the lock.

I closed the door and turned to find her all the way in the living room, heading for my desk. She trailed one finger across the smooth bare wood before she turned on the lamp there, as well.

It struck me as odd—forward for the woman who'd hesitated accepting my offer of a simple jelly croissant and coffee to strut so boldly through my home. But, hey, I was all for her making herself comfortable in my place.

Hopefully, she'd want to stay here awhile.

When she nudged the pile of mail with a fingertip, sending the neat stack of envelopes on the desk sprawling, her visual perusal changed to actual physical rifling through my stuff.

She glanced up and saw me watching her. With a smile she left the desk behind and headed straight for me.

Before I could say or do anything, she'd fisted my lapels and pulled me toward her lips.

Then we were kissing. Not a gentle kiss either. This was a full mouth, tongue-tangling, soul-deep kiss that I hadn't started but which I was more than willing to continue.

I braced my hands on her waist, partly to keep my balance as she pushed against me, partly because I'd wanted to touch her all night.

As she tipped her head and plunged her tongue against mine, I slid my palms down to cup her ass.

She moaned and that had my semi turning rock hard.

The sinfully high heels boosted her height enough I didn't have to bend too far to reach what I wanted—that being her mouth and her firm ass.

But this would be so much more enjoyable for both of us if we were horizontal.

I broke the lip lock and gazed down at this enigma of a woman. Her lips were parted slightly as her chest rose and fell with her rapid breaths. Her eyes, heavily lidded, seemed a bit out of focus.

"Shall we take this someplace more comfortable?" It sounded like the cheesiest of lines. I hated that those trite predictable words had even come out of my mouth, but I seemed to have lost all my smooth moves somewhere between Manhattan and Jersey.

In spite of my sounding ridiculous, she nodded. "I'd love to."

Then she was on the move again, leading me toward my own bedroom. I supposed it wasn't that hard for her to determine where it was located. There was only one hallway and the door at the end of it was open to reveal the view of my king-sized bed, which luckily was made thanks to a visit from Antonela today.

The wet towel from the shower I'd taken after work before leaving for dinner with Alex was still hanging on the closet doorknob, but she didn't give it a second glance. She was too busy reaching for my belt.

This was happening and it seemed I didn't have to do a whole lot except participate.

I liked to be in control. I wasn't such a great follower, but tonight, in this situation, I predicted that would change.

Nope, I'd have no problem letting Alex get me naked and lead me to bed. No problem at all.

The way she looked in that dress, and how I anticipated she'd look without it, I couldn't imagine any heterosexual single man wanting to fight this woman.

I don't think I could say no to her even if I'd wanted to and I certainly did not want to.

With her help, my suit ended up on the floor, a place it had never been before, and I didn't even care.

When Alex shoved me, sending me falling backward onto the mattress, I let her, happy to have a good spot from which to enjoy the show happening right in front of me.

She slid off the red dress as deftly as any professional stripper, but she did it with a hell of a lot more class.

I had to swallow and remember to keep breathing when, like a jigsaw puzzle, piece by lovely piece of her was revealed to me, until the whole tempting picture was exposed.

Alex in that dress had been breathtaking. Alex naked was enough to have me struggling for breath.

Bared and beautiful, she crawled onto the bed and straddled my legs.

I'd been braced on my elbows so I could watch her, but I eased back flat now as she hovered above me.

There was one thing she hadn't done and it was something I wanted very much. I reached up and slid my fingers into her hair, which was still up. Constrained, when I wanted it free.

"May I?" I asked.

Alex didn't answer, but reached up with both hands and released her hair for me.

She was like a dream come true, a goddess as her long chestnut hair tumbled down. It just brushed the tops of her breasts, which were high and firm and so tempting I couldn't resist them. I pulled her toward me so I could take one tight peak into my mouth.

I felt her skin, warm and smooth, beneath my palms. The muscles of her back moved beneath my hands as she bracketed my head with her forearms, leaned low, and allowed me to feast on her as I pulled her other nipple into my mouth.

My length brushed between her legs as she gyrated against me. The heat of her body beckoned. Irresistible, so I didn't resist.

I pierced her wet warmth with my tip and then stilled. I had been happily losing myself in the moment, and in this woman, until reality hit me.

That I had enough sanity left to pull myself out of the ecstasy and not plunge inside her unprotected was a miracle.

She was on top, pinning me down.

Unable to move to take care of things myself, I told her, "Condoms are in the drawer."

While still seated astride me, she reached for the bedside table, stretching her long strong body like a cat in the sun.

I had a moment to appreciate that body.

The muscles in her arms and back were defined—muscular—even though she was lean and toned. Her thighs were obviously strong. I could see and feel that.

I wondered what her workout routine was. When she tore into the condom with her teeth, my wondering ceased.

Oh, I still appreciated her body, but it had less to do with her fitness and so much more to do with the fact she had covered me and was slowly easing down over my length.

The sensation had my eyes closing, just when I really wanted to watch. I forced my lids open and watched her move over me.

The way she set her jaw, the fire flashing in her eyes, I would have said she looked angry if we weren't in the midst of an intimate act she'd initiated in the bed she'd led me to.

Alex attacked the act with a vigor that bordered on violence, her expression determined, her movements anything but gentle and I loved it.

I reached out to try to bring her some pleasure

but working her clit at this point would have been akin to performing surgery on a ship tossed about on the ocean during a storm—futile. Possibly dangerous.

I had plenty of time to even the score later.

For now, I wasn't about to waste her passion. If she wanted it rough, fast and hard, that worked for me.

I let myself ride the wave that was Alex for as long as I could before the telltale tingle shot through me.

The speed and force of our combined movements brought me to the point of no return. With no turning back, I gripped her hips, thrust upward and came hard. Loud enough I'd probably have to avoid making eye contact with the neighbors in the hallway for the near future.

She had no choice but to slow and eventually stop as I faded fast. But that was fine because now it was my turn to be in control.

I flipped her over easily, but only because she let me. I had a feeling this woman didn't do anything she didn't want to do.

Again I appreciated how solid she was built. All hard, toned muscle that made me want to ask what she did for her workouts—later. Much later, because now wasn't the time for words.

As I slid down her body, my mouth was about to become very busy and not from talking.

She watched me. Eyes partially closed, she looked more like she was seething than aroused.

I never would have thought that my cute Alex, with the girl-next-door looks and the bright sense of humor, would have such an angry-looking sex face.

She bent her knees, spreading her legs wide for me to fit between them, so I kept going.

I wrote off her expression as one of the facts of life. Some people had resting bitch face. Alex had seething sex face.

There was nothing I could do about it except work toward discovering what her orgasm face looked like. That was certainly something to look forward to.

As a goal oriented man I attacked my challenge with hands and mouth.

At the first contact of my tongue against her core, she gasped. I thrust two fingers inside her and heard her expel a sharp breath. I slipped a single saliva-slickened finger back and pressed just the tip into her rear entrance and she jerked her hips up, pressing herself harder against my mouth.

This I could work with. I had her right where I wanted her—nearing the edge of orgasm and I wasn't going to stop my multi-front assault until I'd reached my goal of hearing her shatter from my touch.

I didn't have to wait long. Her muscles clenched until her thighs shook around my head and her body gripped my fingers inside her so tightly I could barely move.

I sucked harder and felt her careen into the abyss.

Her response was more than I could have imagined. She wasn't quiet or shy. Alex let me and my unfortunate neighbors know exactly how much I'd pleased her.

The boost to my male ego had me hard again. She was still quivering when I slipped on a fresh condom, lifted her knees high and plunged inside.

This time I was in charge and I set a slow but intense pace, sliding deep with each stroke, filling her completely.

I watched her face. Her eyes were closed, her expression softer now, as if she were captivated, captured within the intensity of the pleasure.

Then those eyes opened and her gaze collided with mine. Unlike at dinner, she didn't look away.

The intensity of her stare and the level of feelings it awakened in me were almost too much.

I didn't look away. I forced myself not to. To face what I was feeling for her.

Sex was usually just that for me—sex. This— this was something else. This was raw, naked emotion unlike anything I'd ever felt before and I didn't know what the hell to do about it.

Or maybe I did know what to do about it.

Braced above her, I stilled and said, "Can you stay the night?"

"Yes." Her answer was soft and short but it had my chest tightening along with the rest of my body.

"Good." I pounded us both to completion one more time, with her succumbing first and me following swiftly after.

When it was done, I was as winded as if I'd run a marathon. I rolled to the side and tried to catch my breath.

Once I had some semblance of normalcy back, I settled in close against her. So close we were pressed together, skin to skin, the entire length of our bodies in spite of the sweeping expanse of the king-size mattress.

I wrapped my arms around Alex and held her tight. Needing the connection. Needing to reaffirm to her what I already knew myself—this was no simple hook up. No one-night stand.

This was a beginning.

I could only hope she felt the same.

Her agreeing to stay the night was a good sign. A first step but not an assurance. At least not enough of one for me.

I trailed a finger down the bare skin of her stomach and watched her quiver.

Damn. I wanted to see her come again. Wanted to hear her scream my name. I inched my hand lower into the crease between her thighs. "I can't seem to get enough of you."

Her response was a low indistinct sound as she spread her legs. That was enough of an invitation for me.

I connected with her core and the ride started all over again.

TWELVE

The source of the buzzing barely registered in my sleepy brain as my peaceful slumber ended.

Waking wasn't such a bad thing because as my senses began to become aware, I felt the warm body next to me. She rolled away and I groaned, reaching out to try to pull her back.

Alex did come back soon enough. "Somebody named Zane Alexander is calling you," she said.

I squinted against the morning light and saw the cell phone she retrieved from the nightstand on her side of the bed glowing in her hand.

She thrust the device toward me and I groaned for an entirely different reason now. I was going to have to get out of bed and take this damn call.

"Thanks." I took the phone and sat up, swinging my legs out from under the tangled covers and over the side of the mattress.

Why did Zane insist on calling when he could text instead?

I had a vague memory of shooting him a text at

one point last night asking if he knew where our Russian was going to be this weekend because his female counterpart would be in New York for the event at the Museum of Modern Art.

Even though this crack of dawn phone call was probably my own doing, I still chose to be annoyed at him.

I slipped out of the bedroom and closed the door behind me so I wouldn't disturb Alex any further before I answered the call.

"Dude, you can't wait until the sun is up to bother me?" I dispensed with pleasantries given the hour.

Zane let out a short laugh. "Wow, you're in a mood. For your information, the sun has been up for two hours. What's wrong? You strike out last night? Cranky you didn't get laid?"

It was petty and childish and definitely not gentlemanly behavior on my part but I couldn't resist correcting him. "Wrong on both counts."

"Really? Well, then there's no reason for you to be acting like such an ass—oh. Wait. She's still there." There was far too much amusement in Zane's tone for my liking.

And why the fuck was he so awake and chipper this early on a Saturday morning. I remembered he was married now. That had to be it. He probably had been sound asleep by nine p.m. last night.

With that justification making me happy, I said, "Not that it's any of your business but yes. Why are you calling so early?"

"Dude, it's not that early. I already ran five miles and had breakfast."

I scowled at his level of energy. "Because you have no life."

"Because I'm not out catting around like you."

"You would be if you hadn't found Missy." I glanced back at the closed bedroom door and wondered why I was standing on the wrong side of it fighting with Zane when I could be back in bed making love to Alex. "Can we continue this debate when I'm back in Virginia?"

"And when will that be?" he asked.

"I'm not sure. Probably Monday." I chose to assume my weekend was going to continue on the same tract—me and Alex and my bed with brief interludes for sustenance and to show our faces at the fundraiser. "I can get the comm unit back to you then."

"I'm not worried about the comm. I'm concerned about that cryptic text you sent me."

My guess had been correct. I'd inflicted this torturous conversation on myself by texting Zane last night. My one-time assignment for him might be over but I still felt the responsibility of it weighing on me.

"I'm attending another event in the city tonight. One Viktoria Mikhelson will be at as well. I just wanted to make sure Mordashov wasn't back in the country."

"I'll check it out. As far as I know he's still in the UK but as I told you before, your debt to me is paid. You don't have to worry anymore. You're done, Rosebud."

I sighed, really regretting my code name idea more with every conversation I had with Zane. I should have known better. He never could resist an opportunity at mockery. Not as a kid and obviously not now.

"You're a dickhead. You know that?"

"I love you too, bro. Oh, and why don't you take the comm with you to this event tonight."

"What?" I hadn't even gotten around to making coffee yet but I was wide awake now, on alert as Zane did a one-eighty. He said he wasn't concerned about the Russian. That I was done with my assignment for him. But his telling me to wear the comm to the event told another story.

"Why?" I asked. "Do you think something big might go down?"

He laughed. "No, I don't think *something big might go down* because we're not inside an episode of *Hawaii Five-0*. But it doesn't hurt to be prepared. You might have something interesting to tell me."

Every muscle in my body tensed. Zane might joke around—a lot—but in the middle he'd casually sneak in something vitally important, like he had just now.

It was almost as if he'd hoped I wouldn't notice. Wouldn't question it. That I'd just take the comm and roll with whatever happened next.

The SEAL on the phone with me might be able to do that. But since I was just a normal man, not one of the nation's elite warriors, I wasn't so sure I could.

"Brent, seriously, I'm not worried. I promise you."

"Then why do you want me to carry the comm?"

"Because it's better to have and not need, than to

need and not have."

That philosophy, worthy of Doctor Seuss in its delivery, contained way too many words for me to untangle at the moment.

As I sifted through his meaning, Zane continued, "Won't it make you feel better to have it on you?"

"Yes." That was one thing I was certain of.

"So there you go. Take it with you."

"I will. But I'm not taking the gun."

"Agreed. Concealed carry restrictions in Manhattan can be tricky."

At least I'd won one battle with him. "Will you get back to me if you find out anything new about the Russian's location?"

"I will."

"All right." I glanced again at the door. "I'll, uh, talk to you later?"

"Yeah, that's fine. Go ahead. Get back to whoever she is warming your bed."

I decided to piss him off. "I will. It's Alexandra from the party, by the way."

"What? I told you to steer clear of—"

I was already on my way to the bedroom and too close to the door to say what I wanted to—namely *fuck off*—without Alex hearing from inside the bedroom. Instead I said, "Good bye, Zane."

I disconnected the call before pushing open the door. I startled when I found Alex standing just inside it.

"Hey. Sorry about that." I held up the cell. "Old friend who doesn't respect boundaries when it comes to early calls on weekend mornings."

"It's okay. I figured I'd get up and check my

phone as long as I was awake. Make sure there were no emergencies." She held up her own cell.

"Any volunteer emergencies, you mean?"

"Don't laugh. They happen."

"Well, even volunteers need personal time." I tossed my cell on top of the dresser to free my hands for more important things. Reaching out, I pulled her toward me.

Alex held up one finger. "Hold that thought. I just want to run to the bathroom."

"Of course." I dropped my hold on her waist and watched as she turned, cell still in her hand, and headed for the bathroom.

I didn't think much about that. Sad but true, I'd been known to check my messages while on the toilet.

She'd be back soon enough. Then we'd get back to business.

THIRTEEN

The morning passed too quickly.

Between my dragging Alex back into bed to have sex and then both of us taking showers—separately though I was game to change that in the near future—before I knew it, it was nearing noon.

By the time we got around to eating it was closer to lunch than breakfast and we were within hours of the start of the event, which she still had to dress for.

While we'd been in my apartment, she'd worn a pair of my shorts and a T-shirt. But without any footwear besides the high heels, that outfit wasn't going to work for the drive to her place so she'd put the dress back on.

Not that I minded. I had a real affinity for that red dress, but I'm sure no woman wanted to arrive home the next day wearing the clothes from the night before.

I, on the other hand, was dressed and ready in a

fresh suit as I sat behind the wheel of the Land Rover on the way to Queens and Alex's place.

Out of the corner of my eye I saw her angled toward me, watching me from the passenger seat. Without turning to look directly at her, I said, "You're looking at me strangely. Why?"

"Just trying to figure you out, Brent Hearst."

I glanced her directly, surprised at that answer. "What's there to figure out?"

"I don't know. Everything, I guess." She lifted one shoulder.

"Then that makes us even, because I'm trying to figure you out too, Alexandra . . ." I had started to echo her comment to me but stopped, unable to finish. I laughed. "And I still don't know your last name."

That I'd spent a considerable amount of time inside this woman last night yet didn't know her full name was not ideal. Some men might operate that way. Hell, I had in the past. But not this time. Not with Alex.

I had plans—or at least hopes—to spend much more time with her in the future.

"Jones. Alexandra Elizabeth Jones. And there's nothing to figure out. I go to college, I volunteer. And if I don't get my degree and land a paying job soon my parents are probably going to cut me off and I'll be homeless. I'm pretty typical I think."

"What are you majoring in?" I asked.

"Double major in English and Art History."

Having the Hearst last name could be a double-edged sword at times, but in this situation it might be an asset.

"Lucky for you, I happen to run not one but two publishing houses and I daresay I have some pull at a few other companies."

She laughed. "Hearst owns more than *a few* other companies."

"Oh, so you've heard of them?" I grinned.

Alex let out a snort. "Yeah, you know, in passing."

"All joking aside. Alex, I'd be happy to set you up with some interviews. You just have to tell me what you want."

"What I want . . . I guess that's something I'm going to have to figure out." All humor had gone out of her tone too.

I understood what she was saying. I wasn't *that* much older than she was that I'd forgotten what it was like to be in college. I remembered being fresh out of school, overwhelmed by a world of choices and the prospect of having to pick just one.

"Maybe I can help with that too. We can figure it out together."

"Maybe."

I took my eyes off the road long enough to glance at her. She raised her gaze to meet mine and I saw something in her eyes. Something deep. Dark.

What was that coloring her tone and her expression? It seemed like more than simple indecision.

Whatever it was, I didn't like it.

"You have reached your destination." The GPS announced our arrival at her apartment.

Perfect timing.

I pulled into a spot along the curb and reached

out to squeeze her hand.

Determined to erase that dark cloud that had settled over the woman who was currently the brightest light in my life, I leaned forward and pressed a soft kiss to her lips.

It was short but had a lasting effect on my heart and my head.

A knowledge I wasn't ready for but wasn't going to fight settled over me. I could fall for this woman. Hell, I was already half there.

And God help me if she didn't feel the same.

I pulled back. "Shall we go in?"

A frown creased her forehead. "Would you mind if I went in alone? I feel horrible asking that but the place is a mess and I have a roommate who is a bitch and gets pissy if I bring anyone over. There's a coffee shop right over—"

"Alex, it's fine. I can keep myself busy. You can meet me at the coffee shop when you're ready. Or text me and I'll meet you back here at the car. Your choice."

"That would be perfect. Thank you so much for putting up with me."

"Always." Little did she know I'd do this and so much more for her. "Now go. Get dressed. Do you want me to get you a coffee?"

"No. I'm good. Thanks."

I watched her disappear inside the building, already planning. Wondering. How many more credits did she need to graduate? I'd have to ask. I didn't even know which college she was enrolled in.

There was a lot more to learn, for both of us, but

I had a feeling I'd enjoy finding out everything about her.

So this was what falling for a woman did to a man. Made him feel off balance and centered all at the same time. Content and anxious. Hopeful and frightened.

It was a hell of a thing and I feared I might already be addicted to the feeling.

With a sigh I unhooked my seatbelt and reached into the console for my cell phone.

I figured I could occupy my time at the coffee shop across the street by checking my email on my phone. Or hell, maybe I'd live a little and not cram work into every moment and listen to an audiobook instead.

I smiled. Maybe love was softening up this workaholic.

Or maybe I was just sleep deprived and lazy today. Given that Alex was the reason why I was up half the night, I wasn't going to complain.

I slid the cell into the inside breast pocket of my suit jacket and remembered the communicator there that I'd brought with me on Zane's recommendation.

Could he hear everything now from inside my pocket? Probably. Was he listening? I didn't know.

All I did know was that I wasn't sure I wanted Zane listening in on me—not on my date and definitely not in my apartment while Alex was there.

It was one thing if he overheard certain moments when we'd been roommates at boarding school. But him hearing now that we were adults was quite another story.

Knowing Zane, he probably would listen, just to gather fodder with which to tease me.

Considering that, I'd be very happy to get rid of this thing Monday. I'd hit up his office as soon as I arrived in Virginia rather than wait. I was starting to feel like Big Brother was watching me and I didn't like it.

Inside the coffee shop, I ordered a latte for myself and grabbed a napkin from the dispenser.

An idea hit me and I grabbed another. I'd wrap the damn comm up so tight even if Zane were listening all he'd hear was muffled noise. But I'd still have the unit in case I did need it.

Feeling like a genius from the brilliance of my plan, I carried my coffee and my napkins to a table, settled in a chair and set to work on the satisfying task of smothering Zane's spy device.

I'd completed my task and was still shopping for a good title on the audiobook site when the door swung open, sending the tiny bell attached tinkling. The sound and curiosity had me glancing up.

"Alex." My pulse picked up speed at the sight of her. Pushing aside the knowledge that I had it bad for her already, I said, "I would have met you at the car so you didn't have to walk across the street."

"It's fine. I don't mind the walk."

It looked like she'd put on a bare minimum of makeup but she didn't need any at all to be beautiful, in my opinion.

She'd changed into an ivory colored shirt, wide-leg navy blue pants and shoes slightly less high than the heels she'd worn last night, but still sexy as hell.

Although maybe it was just Alex and not the shoes, because she'd made even my shorts and tee look sexy this morning.

"You look great." I wasn't just saying that to flatter her. She did look great and she'd transformed herself faster than I'd expected. I hadn't even finished my coffee yet. "We have time. You sure you don't want something?" I gestured toward the counter.

"No, thank you. Actually, I wouldn't mind if we got to the event early."

"Oh, okay. Sure. We can go." In fact, I liked that idea.

I grabbed my to-go cup and moved ahead to open the door to the street for her. The sooner we got there, the sooner we could leave and go back to my place.

Another night with Alex. That thought had my spirits soaring.

FOURTEEN

Trying to find street parking anywhere in the vicinity of the museum on a Saturday afternoon was insane.

As I fought the traffic, I remembered one of the key reasons why I no longer lived in Manhattan. I circled the block one more time and then pulled up to the curb in front of the museum.

I flipped on my hazards and turned in my seat to face Alex. "Let me drop you off here in front. I'll go find a spot and meet you inside."

"It's okay. I'll come with you."

"It could take a while. And it might be far."

Lips pressed together, Alex shook her head. "It's fine. I don't mind walking. I can use the exercise."

She didn't need the exercise. She was in top shape as far as I could see—and I'd seen all of her so I knew. But I didn't argue. "All righty, then. If you won't let me be a gentleman, then I'll guess we'll walk."

"I guess we will." She turned to look out the side window and the discussion was over.

Man, she could be stubborn. It didn't make me like her any less but I did anticipate some animated debates between us in future since I had a bit of a hard headed streak myself.

"Just to let you know, if you were wearing those heels you had on last night there'd be no argument. You'd be getting out here and waiting for me inside."

"Luckily, I don't have on the heels from last night."

"Pity." I grinned as visions of her in them flashed through my mind. I saw Alex cock up a brow before I threw the vehicle into drive and glanced over my shoulder to check the traffic.

I finally gave up finding street parking and pulled into a public parking garage on 6th that could take oversized vehicles.

The attendant informed me of the hefty surcharge to park the aforementioned oversized vehicle and I surrendered my keys and my credit card to him.

I didn't even like letting valets park my cars. I liked turning over control of my vehicle to a city parking attendant even less.

In fact, I hated it, but for lack of a better option, I did it anyway and watched my baby disappear up the narrow ramp accompanied by a squeal of tires.

Cringing, I did my best to pocket my concern over the Land Rover and turned my attention back to my date.

Walking in the city, crossing streets and

navigating the crowds and tourists on the sidewalk, was a good excuse to take her hand in mine. I took advantage of the opportunity.

She glanced at me but didn't pull away. I enjoyed the feel of walking hand-in-hand with Alex. The act had a distinct *couple* feel to it.

Since my parking escapade had taken so long, we didn't arrive early, but we did arrive on time. The doors were closed to regular museum visitors, it closed to the public at five-thirty on Saturdays, but it wasn't closed to us.

We entered and checked into the event under *Alexandra Jones and Guest* and were directed to the Collections Gallery by the volunteer.

"It's good you're off duty." I glanced down at Alex as we moved toward the escalator.

"Hm?"

"I'm glad you didn't have to work tonight at the check-in desk."

"Oh. Yeah. Me too."

We reached our floor and I saw immediately we were at the right place, judging by the catering staff and guests intermixed with the modern art.

The first thing I always did at any event was locate the bar. I spotted it surreally set up in front of Van Gough's *Starry Night*.

The placement made for an interesting juxtaposition. Though honestly, after having eaten dinner with a couple of hundred other benefactors beneath the giant whale at the Museum of Natural History, nothing at these fundraisers surprised me anymore.

It was something a person got used to after a few

of these events—partying next to art and antiquities that the general public weren't allowed within a yard of, and definitely not while they had food or drink in their possession.

I turned to Alex and asked, "Something to drink?"

"No, thank you. But you go ahead."

"Okay. I will." I leaned down and pressed a kiss to her cheek and then walked away toward the alcohol, smiling.

Oh, yeah. I could get used to this whole *couple* thing.

The cell phone in my pocket buzzed before I made it past the Monet. I stepped to the side so I'd be out of the flow of traffic also en route to the bar and pulled the phone out of my pocket.

Zane's name on a new text notification had me on alert. I opened his message.

GET ON YOUR COMM

All caps. No pleasantries. No jokes.

None of that was like my old buddy Zane. It was more like the new Zane I'd gotten to know. Zane the SEAL. The security specialist. The guy who owned things like comms and leg holsters.

I reached into my pocket and let out a breath of relief that my coffee shop napkin was still there. I pulled it out and unfolded it to reveal the tiny flesh covered device.

Turning to face the work of art on the wall, I pretended to be studying Monet's *Water Lilies* as I shoved the unit deep into my ear and whispered, "Hello?"

"Can you confirm who you're there with?"

"What do you mean?" I angled my head to glance around. "Lots of people. It's a fundraiser."

I remembered Alex had handed me the event program after we'd checked in. I'd stashed it in my pocket since it wouldn't fit in her small purse. I pulled it out now about to read any names I could find to Zane when he said, "No, I mean your date. Who is she?"

"Alexandra Jones. I told you I was with her this morning. The volunteer from the Hamptons event. Why?"

"Because when I put our computer guy on finding out where Mordashov was this weekend I also gave him your date's name."

"And how did you know her last name since I never told you?" I asked, remembering that I'd only found it out myself this afternoon.

"I heard you talking over the comm."

Shit. I was right. He could hear us on the comm in my pocket and the bastard had been listening. "You mother-fu—"

"Brent. Listen to me. This is important."

I didn't like the tone I heard in my friend's voice. My heart picked up speed as I asked, "What?"

"She doesn't exist."

"What do you mean she doesn't exist? She was sitting next to one of the event organizers in the Hamptons. They called her by name. Then last night, she had two tickets to the charity reading and after party with the damn poet laureate of the United States. And today here at the MoMA she checked in under—"

"Stop ranting and let me finish. That name for

that girl doesn't exist on any public records that we can find."

I glanced up and saw Alex watching me. She probably wasn't the only one. I was starring at a Monet arguing with no one as far as the other guests could see. I needed to move somewhere private.

Catching Alex's eye, I forced a smile and motioned toward the men's room.

She nodded and I practically ran for the bathroom.

Inside a stall I figured it was safe to talk. Anyone listening would think I was on the phone.

I was no good at this spy crap. I probably should have whipped out my cell before and pretended to be speaking on it.

But it was better I was in private for this disturbing conversation anyway.

I turned my focus back to straightening out this mess with Zane. "I drove her to her apartment today. In Queens. Check this address." I was about to relay the street and building number I'd parked in front of to Zane.

I didn't have time before he said, "I already checked out that location this afternoon. Nothing."

I frowned. "How could you have checked this afternoon?"

"Your comm has GPS. I saw you hanging out in Queens today while this whole Alexandra thing was breaking so I had my guy specifically check out that area. There's no evidence of her there either."

"She said she has a roommate. Maybe Alex's name isn't on the lease."

"Did you go inside the apartment?" he asked.

"No." I shook my head, not believing any of this.

She had to live at the apartment in Queens. She went inside wearing one set of clothes and came out in a completely different outfit.

But his silence in response to my answer spoke volumes.

He really believed I'd had the wool pulled over my eyes by this woman I was possibly falling for.

It was crazy.

What Zane was saying couldn't be true. I just had to convince him of that.

"She's a student. She said she's getting close to graduating. Check students enrolled in classes in the area."

"Which school?" he asked.

"I don't know. Check all of them in the five boroughs. Hell, check Yonkers and the southern suburbs too. Or maybe she's taking classes online. Can your guy check enrollment for those too?"

"He's on it now, but Brent, you need to face the fact she might be lying to you. She isn't who she says she is.

Shit. I was beginning to realize exactly how little I knew as far as cold hard facts about Alex's life, but that didn't matter because I knew *her*. Intimately, in fact.

"Zane. That can't be. We spent the night together." I hissed that last detail, low but with fervor. It was an important detail.

"That doesn't mean anything."

"No, you're wrong." I shook my head. "You don't understand. It wasn't a hookup or a one-night stand. We had coffee together in Montauk. We had dinner last night before the reading. We spent all day today together. We've been holding hands, for God's sake."

"Brent, that's what they do. She's been grooming you."

I shook my head, unable to believe what I was hearing. "Why? What could I possibly have that she wants—" It hit me. "You think she's after my money?"

"Possibly. Or worse."

"Worse? What could be worse?"

"What if she's after something else that you're involved with?"

"Like what? Hearst Corp.?" I was one of many board members, and part of an even larger family. I had no sway over votes or acquisitions.

But she did know my name and my public net worth and had since the moment I stepped up to that check-in table in the Hamptons and announced it to her.

"Brent, corporate espionage is a reality."

"Jesus." I'd always been careful of gold diggers. Always took care of birth control myself to prevent any paternity claims. But corporate espionage?

Would someone really pretend to like me just to get corporate secrets? That was something I'd never considered and certainly hadn't planned for.

"I don't believe that's what Alex is doing. But just in case I'm mistaken and until I can prove to you I'm not, what do you suggest I do?"

"Pretend nothing's wrong but be on alert. Reveal nothing to her. And don't leave her alone with any of your papers or electronics."

"I have a log-in code on my computer."

"Pfft. Passwords are child's play for a real expert."

I covered my face with my hand, unable to believe this was happening to me.

Maybe I didn't have to believe it because there was still the very good chance that Zane was wrong.

"You have the gun on you?" he asked.

"No. You told me not to." I had been trying to keep my voice low, but it was hard to after that question.

"I know. It's fine."

I laughed, because right now nothing seemed fine. "Then why did you ask that question?"

It wasn't as if I was going to shoot Alex for lying to me even if I did have the gun with me.

"Because there's always the possibility that she has something to do with the Russians."

Another theory? I was starting to think my friends had gone off the deep end. He was seeing conspiracies everywhere.

"How? You said the Russian isn't even in the country."

"Correct. But you said Viktoria is going to be there. And she and Mordashov were together in the Hamptons. And so was Alexandra. So . . ."

"So there could be a deeper connection between them all." I drew in a deep breath. "Okay. I'll keep my eyes open and my comm in."

"There's my good Rosebud."

"Not the time to joke."

"I disagree. You need to relax. Or at least look as if you are."

"I'll pull it off. You of all people know the infallibility of my poker face."

"I do, when you're playing cards. What I'm not so sure of is your ability to handle this alone if shit goes sideways."

I blew out a short breath. "Me either. Hopefully we won't have to find out."

"Hopefully. Oh, and Brent, if Alex is going to remain in the dark that we suspect something, you have to act normal around her."

"You already said that. Poker face. Remember?"

"I'm talking about the sexual relationship between you two. Continue exactly as you have been. She wants to blow you in the car on the drive home, you let her."

"Jesus, Zane." I ran my hand over my face.

"I'm serious."

Sadly, I believed he was, but that wasn't the only thing that surprised me. What was the big surprise was that the picture Zane had painted—of Alex and me doing *that*—had me getting hard as a rock.

I still wanted her.

Even with all the doubt, even though my hands were shaking, I wanted her.

If she strode in here right now, hopped up on the counter between the sinks and told me to fuck her, I would.

Gladly.

Because more than wanting her, I still cared. Now as much as ever, in spite of the suspicions Zane had raised.

And what the hell did I do about that?

FIFTEEN

I went back out to the event and bee-lined directly for the bar. If ever I needed a drink, it was now.

Zane might disagree. Hell, if my head was on straight I would too, but it wasn't.

Nothing was straight. Everything was off kilter as my formerly happy world tilted.

"What can I get for you?" The bartender leaned toward me to be able to hear my reply over the noise of the thickening crowd.

I glanced past him at the selections and nearly cried when I saw they had a full selection of top shelf bourbon.

"Hudson. On the rocks."

He nodded and grabbed a glass.

It was as if I was distracted and hyper-observant all at once. I heard the sound of the metal scoop hit the ice and the ice fill the glass.

My thoughts were all over the map. My mind

pinging wildly like signals off a cell tower.

I was aware of the other patrons. One woman had on far too much perfume and one old guy was speaking much too loudly.

I had to fight the urge to touch the comm in my ear and make sure it wasn't showing.

Meanwhile, I kept one eye on the escalator to see who was arriving, especially keeping watch for Viktoria, who might possibly be a target.

A target for what and from whom I still didn't know.

Hell, Zane didn't even know where the threat would come from, if it came at all.

How had I gotten involved in this shit?

Oh yeah, that's right. I let Zane do me a favor.

That would never happen again. From now on if that man did anything for me I was paying his going rate and asking for a receipt to confirm there was no debt owed.

"Everything all right?"

I was wound so damn tight, the sound of Alex's voice close behind me made me jump. I forced myself to turn slowly and smile down at the face of the woman I'd been picturing a future with just a few hours ago.

"Everything is fine. They have my favorite brand of bourbon so I'm more than fine." I hoped the joke would mask my nerves.

Act normal. The specter of Zane's warning haunted me.

What would normal me do? The Brent who didn't suspect his date of being a corporate spy if not an international assassin?

115

I knew the answer. He'd lean down and kiss those lips that were still too damn tempting.

Zane's other words of wisdom flew unbidden into my brain.

She wants to blow you, let her.

Jesus. I would too. Because after envisioning that scene it was the only thing I wanted. Her lips wrapped around me.

That couldn't happen here and now as I waited for my drink, but this could—I thrust my hand beneath her hair, pulled her closer, leaned down and kissed her.

She'd left her hair down tonight. I tangled my fingers in her long tresses and really kissed her. No chaste peck on the lips, but a full out, tongue thrusting, completely inappropriate for a public venue kiss.

I didn't know if I was madder at her for possibly being a liar or at myself for not being able to control my desire for her. All I knew was I felt better after crushing her mouth with mine and claiming her with that angry kiss.

"Sir."

The moment ended as quickly as it had begun.

My drink was ready—it didn't take all that long to pour some bourbon over ice—and there was a line of patrons not so patiently waiting behind me as I blocked their way to the alcohol.

I dropped my hold on Alex. Ignoring the shock on her face, I turned away from her and toward the bar.

I took the drink and thanked the bartender as casually as if I hadn't just had my tongue down my date's throat right in front of him and the Van Gough.

This was turning out to be the most surreal night of my life.

"Sure you don't want anything?" I asked Alex, taking a healthy swallow from my glass before she even had a chance to respond.

"No, thank you." She continued to watch me closely.

I was done with her scrutiny. My bourbon muscles making me brave, I laid my arm around her shoulders, angled us both forward and said, "Then let's go mingle."

"Mingle?" she asked.

"Sure. Isn't that what these things are for?"

If she were talking to someone else, I'd have a chance to observe her. Maybe glean some answers to my many questions while she made conversation with the other guests.

That gave me an idea.

"Who do you know from this organization, anyway?" I asked.

"What?" She looked surprised by my question.

"You had two tickets so I assume you have a personal connection to the not-for-profit running this thing."

Her eyes widened and she sputtered.

If she couldn't even answer the simple question of where she'd gotten the tickets something was very wrong.

Holy shit. Was Zane right?

With every fiber of my being I didn't want him to be right. I wanted Alex to be just the struggling college student who liked to volunteer and had dreams of entering the workforce.

But now that I looked at her more closely, there was a level of confidence within her, a strength that was in direct opposition to the other side she liked to trot out for me—that being the shy woman in the red dress who looked uncomfortable accepting a compliment and dodged attention.

I was so stupid. A woman who didn't like attention, the way she pretended not to, would never have worn that dress.

Alex was a honey pot.

Jesus.

It took me a moment, but once I wrapped my head around that concept I realized that made me Winnie the Pooh, the bumbling fool willing to do anything to get me some of her honey.

Somehow mixing characters from a children's story with the sexual game of intrigue we were involved in seemed particularly wrong to me.

Fuck. This whole thing felt wrong to me.

"Brent."

I jumped again as Zane's voice filled my ear.

Did he expect me to answer? Now? Couldn't he hear that I was standing right next to Alex and couldn't reply?

"I'm sending you backup," he continued without waiting for a response. But all his information did was raise more questions in my mind.

Why was he sending backup? Had he learned something new? Was Viktoria in danger? Was I? And who the fuck was he sending to help me?

"I'll let you know when he's in place. It might be

awhile so keep acting normal until I get back to you."

Easier said than done, but at least I knew a bit more than I had before.

Meanwhile, both the conversation and my steps had lagged during the little one-sided conversation in my ear.

I glanced down to find Alex starring at me.

"Sorry. I just realized I forgot to email my assistant in Virginia to tell her that I might not be in until late Monday."

"Oh?" she asked.

I forced a smile I hoped looked genuine. "Yeah. You see, there's a very tempting woman who I was hoping would keep me occupied late tonight, so I'll have to take the train on Monday morning instead of tomorrow."

Her gaze met and held mine and in her eyes I imagined I saw emotion that actually looked genuine. This woman was either the best actress on the planet or Zane was very wrong.

Or maybe there was a third option.

Perhaps she was as confused as I was, physically craving this person in front of me more than I'd ever wanted a woman in my life—wanting her to be the kind of person I'd believed her to be—all in spite of the evidence that she might well be working against me.

Fuck it.

I downed the remainder of the drink and ditched the glass on a nearby tray. Then, right there in the middle of the bustling crowd, I grabbed Alex's face between my palms, stepped in close to her body and took possession of her mouth one more time.

If I was Winnie the Pooh in this scenario, I intended to gorge myself on the honey pot in my hands.

I'd worry about the consequences later.

SIXTEEN

Alex broke away from the kiss first. Her lips were swollen, her breath coming fast. I took great masculine satisfaction in that.

Even if she was faking all the rest, this—this desire I aroused in her with just a kiss—was genuine.

Then again, what the hell did I know? My judgment was definitely in question at this point.

"I think you were right. We probably should wander around and mingle . . . before we cause a spectacle," she said.

I snorted as I glanced around us. I saw more than a few stares and looks of censure. "I think it's a bit late for that, but sure. Let's wander."

Suspicious, confused and aroused, my mind spun like a roulette wheel, finally landing on what Alex had said when she'd told me about this event last night—back when I still trusted her.

Oh how things had changed in such a short time.

"I thought Viktoria was supposed to be here." My comment elicited a strong reaction in Alex, just as I feared it would.

She whipped her head around to look at me. "I did. Why do you ask?"

Was this her game? Was Zane right in that this mess could be something to do with the Russians?

I couldn't wrap my head around it. But then again, this was my first case of international intrigue that didn't come off the pages of a novel or from a movie screen.

I lifted my shoulder in a shrug with as much nonchalance as I could muster.

"No reason. Just wondering. You were the one who brought her up yesterday. Not me. In fact, you pointed it out specifically. Remember?" There was an edge to my tone I couldn't hide.

Maybe I'd better stop talking. I might have a poker face, but apparently I couldn't keep my emotions out of my spoken words for shit.

My anger and hurt was seeping out in spite of Zane's warning. I had to rein in my emotions.

Trying to undo any damage I turned to face Alex. "Okay, the truth? One of my publishing houses puts out an online magazine. The target market is millennial women. I was hoping Viktoria might consent to an interview."

She watched me, as if evaluating the truth of my words.

I didn't blame her for that. What I'd just told her was a complete lie. And I had been acting pretty strange today. At least I had been since my little discussion with Zane.

"Backup is on site." Zane's voice in my ear startled me one more time.

Dammit, I needed to stop jumping every time he talked to me.

The minute this bullshit was over and I could speak to him freely I was going to make a few suggestions about the whole comm procedure.

First and foremost would be some sort of warning beep or click or something so the person wearing the comm didn't get a blast of words in their ear as they were trying to act normally while under the close scrutiny of a possible international spy.

Could that really be what Alex was? Some sort of undercover operator? It would explain the fact that she was in better shape than I was—and I should know since I'd had all of her limbs wrapped around me very recently.

God, how I wanted that again.

For maybe the first time ever I got why James Bond would screw the brains out of a woman and not consider—or maybe just not care—that in the next scene she was going to try to kill him.

Truth was stranger than fiction sometimes. My feelings for Alex were my truth in spite of the fact it seemed our relationship was her fiction.

Christ, I was getting sappy and poetic in my heartbreak. Or maybe it was just the bourbon.

Meanwhile, I didn't know who this backup from Zane was or where he would be, and Alex was still watching me like I was insane, probably because our conversation had ground to a halt.

I obviously wasn't a good multi-tasker. I

couldn't juggle Zane in my ear, my own thoughts in my head and still make stimulating small talk with my date at the same time.

Though if I remembered correctly, the conversational ball was in Alex's court since I'd lobbed the last shot, serving up my excuse for looking for Viktoria.

"You're right. She was supposed to be here." Alex glanced around us, then back to me. "Will you excuse me while I go to the ladies room?"

"Of course." I welcomed it, in fact.

Her leaving me meant I could head to the Monet for another conversation with the *Water Lilies* and Zane.

The moment Alex and her tempting ass—Christ, I really did have issues when it came to her—disappeared into the bathroom, I turned toward the wall.

"Zane! What backup? Who? Where? And why do I need it?"

"Whoa. Slow down, Rosebud. Just a precaution."

If he was mocking me again the situation couldn't be that dire. Maybe I could believe him when he said he was just being cautious.

"No GAPS guys were in Manhattan. But luckily a friend of mine happened to be there. He's in the building with you."

"How will I recognize him?"

"You don't need to. He'll find you. He's just there as overwatch."

Overwatch.

I felt like I needed a dictionary of military terms while speaking with Zane but I got the gist. This guy would be watching over me in case I needed help. But I still didn't know why.

"What are you worried about?" I asked.

"Besides your lying date?" He snorted. "The fact Viktoria Mikhelson has gone missing is a bit concerning."

"What?" So her absence was something to worry about. "You know that for a fact or are you assuming that because I haven't spotted her yet?"

"I know she arrived at the museum half an hour ago, entered the front door and isn't up there with you at the party."

"Maybe the director of the museum took her on a private tour. Or to a meeting somewhere."

"Maybe." He sounded doubtful.

"Why would anyone want to grab her?"

"Maybe it's not her. It could be her date."

This was new. Yet another thread in my rapidly unraveling world. "What date? Who is it?"

"Not sure. We're trying to identify him from the image we grabbed off the street camera outside the museum. He arrived with Viktoria at seventeen-thirty-five."

I hesitated as I checked my watch to see what time it was now.

"That's five thirty-five, Rosebud."

"I know. I was checking the time, dickhead." I glanced up and saw the shocked glance I got from a fellow art lover who was standing nearby and had obviously overheard me.

I cringed. In my frustration I'd thrown caution, and whispering, to the wind and had spoken too loudly.

"Sorry. Bluetooth earpiece." I pointed to my ear and then cut my losses by turning and walking away. In the corner of the room, I pulled my phone out of my pocket and held it in my hand to further sell the lie that I was speaking on a normal cellphone ear bud and not some piece of military grade, Spec Op-approved equipment.

I didn't know if there were rules about cell phone usage in the museum, but at the moment I didn't care.

"So what do I do?" I asked Zane.

"For now, just keep your eyes and ears open. I'll let you know if anything changes."

Once again I was nothing but a human security camera inside an event to feed the action to Zane off-site. I was getting pretty tired of being involved while at the same time not really being involved at all.

"Who are you talking to?"

I whipped around to find that, once again, Alex had snuck up on me. You'd think those heels of hers would make some sort of noise. Maybe they had and I'd been too distracted to notice.

Her gaze dropped to the cell clutched in my hands and then up to my face as she waited for my answer.

"My friend Zane." I made a show of holding up the phone and then said, "Gotta go, buddy. Call you later." I hit the screen that had no call on it and pocketed the cell again.

"You using your prototype ear bud?" she asked, staring at my ear.

"Yup."

Her focus remained intensely upon me. "I thought the battery was dead and you had to return it."

"I charged it. I can't mail it back until I go to the post office on Monday so I figured I'd use it." That had slipped out pretty effortlessly.

Was I getting better at lying?

Practice makes perfect, or so they say, and it certainly seemed I was telling more lies than truths since meeting Alex.

That was no way to start a relationship, even if it did turn out that she was possibly a fake and a liar herself.

When she nodded, I breathed in relief she'd bought my story.

"Would you mind if we stepped outside just for a few minutes and got some air? I'm feeling a bit claustrophobic in here." Alex pressed a hand to her chest.

The MoMA, and the space where we were in particular, had an open floor plan, all painted a minimalist white to highlight the art. But the event had filled up and there was a press of people in our area, mostly because we'd never gotten very far from the bar.

"Sure." I nodded. "Some air sounds good."

And it would give me the opportunity to explore more of the space, see if I could spot Viktoria or anything out of the ordinary to report to Zane.

She headed for the elevator rather than the escalator, which would have given me more of a view.

We were all the way up on the fifth floor, and

without a good reason to redirect her away from using the elevator I had no choice but to follow. When the doors swooshed open, I stepped inside the elevator car after her.

She leaned forward and punched the button for the lowest level.

I had assumed we'd exit the way we'd come in, through the main entrance, but I knew for a fact the museum had multiple exits and maybe the one she'd chosen offered a better place to get some air than 54th Street. It wouldn't be hard to improve upon that.

When the elevator doors opened again, it was to reveal a darkened interior floor that was definitely not a place to get some air.

It didn't even look like an area we were allowed to be.

In fact, it looked like a good spot to be killed without anyone ever hearing a thing and I really didn't want to be there with Alex . . . or whoever she was.

Shit.

SEVENTEEN

I remained inside the elevator. I turned away from the open door and the yawning cavern of darkness it had revealed and faced her.

"Where are we?"

"The theater level."

The space looked completely deserted, dark except for a few scattered security lights that cast an eerie red glow.

Ignoring everything that told me we shouldn't be here, Alex exited the elevator, leaving me still standing inside wondering what to do next.

Alex reached back and pulled me by the hand. "Come on."

Nothing about this felt right.

Maybe if I didn't suspect her, then yeah, fine, I'd be all over doing the nasty in the deserted theater while the party goers continued unaware floors above us.

But given what I knew from Zane, this felt more

like a good place to be murdered than a place for getting naughty.

Zane.

I realized I wasn't alone. I could tell him where I was *if* the comm worked all the way down here. Did it?

I decided to find out. "This T-Level you brought us down to is pretty deep underground. I mean we're two floors beneath the main lobby level. I wonder if there's even any cell signal all the way down here."

I threw as many hints in Zane's direction as I thought I could get away with.

"I copy." For once, Zane's voice in my ear was welcome, until Alex narrowed her eyes and glared at me.

She held out her hand palm up. "You can just hand over that comm right now."

My eyes widened. "Excuse me?"

What the hell? How did she know? And who the hell was she that she was talking more like one of Zane's covert operatives than a college student or a volunteer?

"That communicator in your ear. I figure you got it from your friend Zane Alexander. It looks like something a SEAL turned mercenary would use."

"Fu—why does everyone think I'm a fucking mercenary?" Zane's voice came through loud and annoyed.

He was bothered by *that*?

How about the fact I was alone and in a very precarious situation with a woman who was starting to scare me and was now about to take my communicator so I'd be cut off from my only support?

"Zane's just a friend. We went to school together . . . and he's not a mercenary." I threw him that bone, hoping he'd be satisfied and concentrate on getting me out of this situation instead of obsessing over semantics.

"Maybe. Maybe not. But that still leaves the question of who you are and who you're working for." Apparently tired of waiting for me to turn over the comm, Alex took a step closer. "Give it or I'll take it."

I was starting to get pissed.

Who could blame me? This was turning into the worst date of my life.

I'd probably end up dead and buried beneath the Abby Aldrich Rockefeller Sculpture Garden if the hate-filled glare Alex had leveled on me was any indication, but I didn't give in.

Folding my arms across my chest, I said, "No."

"Fine, have it your way."

A step, a reach, a twist and the next thing I knew I was flat on my back with the wind knocked out of me, gasping for breath as Alex straddled me.

She poked a finger into my ear none too gently. With satisfaction she held up the comm, peering at in by the glow of the exit sign.

"It is a nice piece of equipment, I'll admit. Too bad I have to do this."

Still sitting on me, she took off one shoe, put the comm on the floor and smashed it.

I watched in shock, unable to stop her. "What are you doing?"

"Disabling your means of communication with your *friend*." With the deadly looking heel still clutched in her hand and poised above my eye, she said, "Tell me who you work for and what your assignment is."

She wouldn't do it. She couldn't do it. Could she? Kill me with a high heel?

Was it even possible? Even if I didn't die, I had no doubt she could blind me with that thing.

Did her wielding the heel at me mean she didn't have another weapon? Did she not have a gun on her?

That thought made me brave and I said, "How about you tell me who you work for."

She lifted a brow and I wondered if my bravado had impressed her or if she was just thinking I was an idiot who deserved to die.

The sound of the elevator rumbling to a stop and the door opening sent both of our heads swiveling in that direction.

I didn't know whether to be relieved or worried when a man stepped off the elevator, gun first.

"Another one?" She sighed. "Who the fuck are you?"

It was my turn to wonder if she was brave or stupid. After all, she was the one bringing a shoe to a gunfight.

"I do fancy hearing a naughty word from the lips of a beautiful female now and again. Don't you, Brent?"

The man with the accent that made him sound like British royalty knew my name?

I answered his question, though chances were

good it had been purely rhetorical. "Yes. Usually."

He had to be my backup, but where the hell had Zane found this guy?

In an obviously bespoke suit that fit him like a glove and with a face that was made for modeling, he looked more as if he'd stepped out of GQ Magazine than the GI ranks . . .Well, except for the gun, of course.

I didn't know who he was but boy was I glad to see him and his gun.

"MI6?" Alex asked.

I frowned at her question to the man. MI6? Like James Bond?

The stranger smiled. "That obvious?"

"Sorry to blow up your delusions, but yeah. It is." She shrugged.

How come I seemed to be the only one in the dark here? Feeling clueless was getting annoying. And how was Alex so calm with a gun pointed at her?

"Now, let me guess what you are, Alexandra. I'd put money on KGB, if I were a betting man."

"KGB?" To my horror, my voice squeaked.

She laughed still looking at him while sitting on me. "Your age is showing. The KGB was replaced by the FSB in 1991."

I noted she never denied his accusation. But she also didn't confirm it. How stupid was I that her omission gave me hope?

"What can I say? I'm old school." The stranger shrugged. "How about you stand up and put your shoe back on—it's lovely by the way. Louboutin?"

"Good eye," she replied.

Her fucking shoes were Christian Louboutin? I knew enough to know that with what those things cost, there was no way she was a struggling college student living off her parents. Not that there could be any doubt left in my mind about that now.

Meanwhile the surreal banter between the British spy and the possible Russian spy continued, as if I weren't even here.

"Thank you." The man nodded. "Now, why don't you get off my friend there."

Finally, someone remembered my existence.

"I'm afraid I can't do that." She shook her head. "And I wouldn't worry about my deadly shoe, if I were you."

"Because of the gun in your leg holster?" he asked. "Don't look so surprised, Alexandra. I can see the bulge through your pants from here. That fabric is much too thin to hide a weapon. You must choose better."

"MI6 training you guys in fashion nowadays?" she asked.

"Just a hobby. Beautiful women in beautiful clothes are a passion of mine."

This conversation would have been entertaining on the big screen accompanied by hot buttered movie popcorn. But from my position on the floor of MoMA's underground theater, I didn't find it amusing.

On top of it all, I was getting pretty damn tired of being bested physically by a woman. Call me chauvinistic. In light of this newest turn of events, I didn't care.

This woman was supposed to be my civic-minded, college student girlfriend. Instead she was some jujitsu expert who'd taken me down with one move and was threatening me with a shoe that cost more than the rent on that apartment she supposedly shared in Queens.

And now I was being rescued by a Bond wannabe.

The whole night had been humiliating and I was tired of it.

I'd wrestled in middle school. I was pretty good at it too, until my growth spurt hit and I got too tall for the wrestling team and started playing basketball instead. But I'd bet I still had some moves.

I counted down from three in my head, then gripped Alex's arms and flipped her over so she was on her back and I was on top of her.

My new dominant position felt much better.

True, I was still confused. I didn't know if I wanted to fuck her or turn her over to the police—possibly both, but being in control was an enormous improvement.

"All right. All this witty spy banter is over. You, Mr. GQ. You first. You got a name?" I asked.

"I do." His lips twitched with a smile. "Tristan Fairchild, at your service."

"I'm assuming Zane sent you."

"He did. I owed him one."

I laughed out loud at the irony of that. "Don't we all."

I turned back to Alex. "Now you. What the fuck, Alex? Who are you and what do you want?"

She cocked a brow. "What I want is to know who you are."

"You know that. I'm Brent Hearst. You know it's true." For better or worse, I was too damn famous to lie about it.

"I know your name. What I don't know is who you're working for and why you show up wherever Viktoria Mikhelson happens to be."

I frowned. "Viktoria? You think I'm after her?"

"Aren't you? Who sent you? What are you supposed to do? Kidnap her? Seduce her?" She narrowed her eyes on the last accusation.

I laughed. "Oh, no, sweetheart. You're the honey pot here, not me."

From off to the side, Tristan chuckled.

Lovely. So glad I'd amused him.

I kept my attention on Alex. "Why do you think I was sent after her?"

"You get a last minute invite to the event in the Hamptons that she was also a last minute addition to. You spent most of the night watching her. You're wearing a comm tonight and reporting in to someone on the other end. There's no question in my mind you were sent because of her. The only question is why and where is she now?"

Shit. Could I tell her the truth? Without Zane's guidance I had to make a judgment call. "I was at that party to keep an eye on Alexey Mordashov. To make sure he didn't get hurt. He just happened to be standing with Viktoria."

She frowned. "Why? You're no bodyguard."

"No kidding. And to answer your question, Zane Alexander owns a security company. Somebody hired him to watch over Alexey while he was in the States."

"And he chose *you* to do it?" The shock in her voice was starting to be insulting.

I wasn't that bad at this job. Jeez. "I wasn't the only one. I was just the only one inside the party. And the reason is because I, too, owed him one."

I heard Tristan laugh once again. "Dangerous position, that."

"So true," I agreed without looking at him. My focus remained on Alex. "So, now you know all my secrets, and I'll probably have to deal with Zane for telling you all of his. Now it's your turn. Who are you? Who do you work for?"

And why did you sleep with me and make me care about you?

I couldn't bring myself to voice that final question aloud even if it was as important as the other two in my mind.

"Viktoria's father hired me to guard her."

"If that's true, you didn't do a very good job of it. She seems to be missing." Tristan's observance had Alex scowling.

She blew out a frustrated breath. "That's because I've been on the wrong trail." She whipped her gaze from Tristan to me. "Chasing you."

"If you'd been honest with me from the beginning, you wouldn't have been chasing me and wouldn't have lost Viktoria."

I had no proof she was really working for Viktoria's father, yet I was all too willing to grasp at the possibility. To cling to the hope. I hated myself for that.

I moved to get off her. It hurt too much to be this close to her. In this position it was too easy to remember our time together—and that it had all been a lie.

I remembered what Tristan had said about her leg holster and reached down before taking my weight off her.

I felt the warmth of her smooth skin against my fingers as I slid my hand up beneath her pants leg. I was trying to disarm a woman who might possibly do me or Viktoria harm and all I could do was remember the feel of her naked beneath me.

Christ. I was a mess.

Getting my head back in the game, I managed to get her weapon out of the holster and then stood.

"I'll just hold on to this." I kept the gun in my hand and glanced at Tristan. "So what's next? What do we do about finding Viktoria? She crushed my comm so I don't have Zane in my ear any more telling me what to do." I tipped my head toward Alex, who was now standing up.

I took a step back to a safe distance and kept a tight grip on the gun in my hand. Better safe than sorry.

"Quite all right. I still have him in my ear. And you're correct. He isn't happy you told your girl everything."

"He'll live." And maybe he'd think twice before sending me to do a job I was so obviously ill equipped to perform.

My cell vibrated in my pocket. I had my suspicions regarding whom it was, which is why I ignored it, not bothering to even check the caller ID.

"Alexander says to, and I quote, answer your damn phone." Tristan smiled after confirming my guess regarding the identity of the caller was correct.

Rolling my eyes, I reached into my pocket, scowled at the display and answered the call.

"Yes?"

"I found her."

"Who? Viktoria?"

"No. Alexandra. I found out who she really is. A photo search finally delivered a match. Her last name is definitely not Jones and she works for—"

"Viktoria's father." I finished his sentence. "She told us."

"No. That was another lie. She's Blackwater."

I'd walked to the other side of the hall and was facing the far wall to get some privacy, but I turned back now.

As more lies piled up, one on top of another, I decided it was safer to not turn my back on this woman.

In fact, I was probably lucky I'd lived through the night we'd spent together because each revelation proved to be more sinister than the next.

"She's what?" I'd heard him the first time, but at this point I wanted confirmation.

"Blackwater. She appears on their payroll."

"Is that information public?" I asked.

"Don't ask questions you don't want the answers to."

All righty, then. So Zane—or more likely his computer guy—had hacked someone's payroll or tax records and that had led them to a private military contractor so notorious even I'd heard of them. And Alexandra worked for them.

"I don't understand. What is she doing here and with me?" From what I knew, Blackwater worked in places like the war zone in the Middle East.

"I can only guess at that but here's what I know. Blackwater's founder Erik Prince, who happens to be Secretary of Education Betsy DeVos's brother by the way, presented a proposal for an off-the-books intelligence arm that reports directly to the Oval Office. That's public knowledge. You can Google it."

If this nightmare ever ended, I would. For now, I had to trust Zane.

He continued, "Now, here's my theory—I don't know how far up the chain of command it goes and at the moment I honestly don't care, but I believe Blackwater has already set up this private spy network and Alex is part of it."

"So she was supposed to be doing what? Watching the Russians? Gathering information?" I asked.

"I don't know. Possibly she's keeping an eye on high level Russian visitors *or* she could be watching for anyone else tailing or making contact with the Russians while they're here."

"Like I was." It was starting to make sense now why she'd zeroed in on me.

"Correct. But the bigger issue is that now Viktoria is missing. She's not with you. She's not with Alex—"

"So where is she?" I finished Zane's thought.

"Exactly."

"We need to find her," I said more to myself than Zane. "But we weren't hired to keep an eye on her.

Just Alexey."

"I contacted the client. They're just as interested in protecting Viktoria at the moment. The original contract has been amended. She's our assignment now."

Things changed fast in this world I'd stumbled into. I'd just have to learn to adapt and roll with it. "All right. So what do we do to find her?"

"You, Tristan and Alex are on site. You need to work together to look for Viktoria."

"Work with Alex? Are you nuts?" I hissed.

"You don't have much choice. Tristan can't work this job alone. You have no experience in the field. She does. She's well trained as far as I can tell and regardless of the details of her assignment, she's just as interested in finding Viktoria as we are. She'll be an asset."

"If she doesn't stab me in the back first."

Oh wait. She'd already done that to me—at least in the metaphorical sense. Might as well add actual injury to the insult.

"Get over it, Rosebud. You got taken in by a pretty face and a hot bod. It happens to the best of us."

"Even you?"

"Even me." Zane's answer made me feel better. "Of course, never on an op."

And now I feel like shit again because I had been fooled while on an assignment. I sighed.

"All right. Let's do this thing." I realized I had no idea what to do or even where to start in our search for Viktoria. "What exactly should I do?"

"Tristan's in charge. He's good. Listen to him.

And try not to let Alex smash your phone the way she destroyed my comm."

She'd almost blinded me with that same shoe. It would have been nice if my friend were a little more concerned about me almost losing an eye than him losing his comm, but whatever. I had other things to worry about.

It seemed I was now answering to James Bond while partnering with my own Bond villain lover. Lovely.

I drew in a breath to steel myself and turned back to look toward the mismatched members of my new team. "I'm hanging up now. Um, over and out."

Zane laughed before the call went dead. Glad he was amused.

Back by the elevators I noticed that not much had changed. Alex was now standing but she was still on the deadly end of Tristan's weapon.

"You gonna keep that on her the whole time we're together?" I asked.

"Does it bother you?" he asked, without answering my question.

"Not at all. Shoot her if you want to. I don't care."

Alex swiveled to frown at me. I was happy she was finally grasping how truly pissed I was now that I knew she'd piled yet another lie on top of the rest.

"You might want to wait though," I continued. "Zane thinks we need her help to find Viktoria."

Tristan's lips twitched at my comment. "Noted."

"Did Zane tell you Daddy didn't hire her. She's Blackwater?"

"I've been informed, yes."

Alex had the nerve to take a step forward. "Brent—"

"Don't. Just don't . . ." I was too mad to even finish a complete sentence. I drew in a breath and started over, abandoning Alex and turning toward Tristan. "Let's just get through this thing. Tristan, you're in charge. Tell us what to do."

He nodded and took a step toward the map posted on the wall next to the elevator. "No doubt there's security cameras set up at the entrance where she was last seen. We'll have to find the room where those cameras feed and get a look at the video for ourselves. I'm guessing that room is located on one of these two lower levels."

"But won't there be a guard in there? What do we do about him?" I truly hoped he didn't say knock him out. I didn't want to be party to doing bodily injury.

Tristan turned from the wall map to smile at me. "Luckily we have an attractive and obviously skilled woman with us to distract him while I'm checking the feed." His gaze hit on Alex.

I was all for using her various skills for good instead of evil, but I didn't think she'd agree.

Surprisingly, she didn't say a word. Her only reply was one small tip of her head.

Maybe she could be a team player after all if it meant getting her to her goal—finding Viktoria.

Or she was just waiting for us to be distracted so she could hit us over the head and run.

I guess we'd know either way soon enough, but I still saw one problem with this plan. Being what I considered an enlightened man, I asked, "What if the guard is a woman?"

Tristan smiled. "Don't sell yourself short, Hearst. I'm sure you'll have no problem stepping in and being a distraction."

My eyes widened as I realized I might have to be the honey pot now and the night turned even more surreal.

Honey Pot: Tales of an Accidental Operative. A Memoir by Brent Hearst.

That thought proved I was losing my mind. But still, the publisher in me couldn't help but think it would make one hell of a best selling title. I batted that errant thought aside to consider later.

Tristan referred to the map one more time. "Judging by the layout, security should be down this hallway." He turned to look at both of us. "Shall we?"

I wasn't turning my back on Alex again anytime soon. I waited for her to follow Tristan and I brought up the rear as my heart pounded.

Enlightened man or not, I prayed the guard was a man as I followed Tristan and Alex down the dim hall into the unknown.

EIGHTEEN

Tristan was good. Even in my terror I could see that. He was well trained. Skilled. Everything I wasn't.

Alex was too. Now that she'd dropped the false persona she'd used with me, she moved like Tristan—like a spy. Quick. Quiet. Cautious.

I could appreciate the skill in him. Seeing it now so clearly in her just made me angry and hurt all over again.

How had I missed all the signs?

I didn't have time to review every place I'd fucked up as Tristan and Alex began to have an entire conversation silently and completely with hand signals.

Not having taken the hand signal class myself, I could only surmise what was happening by the signs they made and how each responded.

When Tristan held up his arm, bent at the elbow, his hand in a fist, Alex stopped immediately.

Bringing up the rear, I did too, just in time before I ran into Alex.

He motioned her forward while he backed away. Tristan headed my direction, grabbed me none to gently, and pulled me into a darkened doorway.

"What's—"

My whisper was cut off by his hand over my mouth. Then I heard it—the reason we had to be so quiet—Alex was in conversation with a man. The guard on duty if I had to guess.

Before I knew it, they were both walking this way, right past our hiding place, all the way back down the long hallway that led to the theater and to the elevator.

Once they were past, Tristan gave me a push in the direction of the room where Alex had met our unsuspecting guard.

Inside the security room he said, "Listen for the elevator or any footsteps. Watch the hallway but stay out of sight."

Shit. I had a job and it sounded like an important one.

I was dying to ask questions but then I wouldn't be able to hear the elevator. Not that I was certain I could even if I were silent since it was quite a distance away.

I stood just inside the doorway, alternating between popping my head out to look into the hall and glancing back at the bank of monitors where Tristan sat punching keys on a keyboard.

"Got her." His triumphant announcement had me blowing out a breath in relief.

I allowed myself to ask a question since he'd

spoken first and his expression as he leaned forward and frowned at the monitor didn't provide me with any answers. "Is it good news or bad?"

"I'm not quite sure as yet." Tristan raised his gaze to meet mine. "But it certainly is interesting."

Since Mister MI6 was being so cryptic, I abandoned my duty of watching the hall to move farther into the room and glance at the monitors.

I saw what looked like a storage room. Likely where the museum kept the pieces of their collection not currently on display.

On the grainy picture I could make out Viktoria. That she was in this area probably wasn't anything to be alarmed about. Nor was the fact she was there with two men. They could be curators showing her a new acquisition for all we knew.

Then again, why were the lights off?

I realized the picture was so bad because we were seeing the image using the camera's night vision. The area was as poorly lit as the theater level we were on was. It appeared only the security lights were illuminated while the overhead lights were off.

Surely if someone was going to show off their collection, they'd want to show it in the best light, literally.

"What do you think's going on?" I asked Tristan, keeping my eye on the screen and the perplexing situation it showed. The three weren't moving. They seemed to be discussing something. "Is it some sort of heist?"

When I heard Tristan chuckle I took my eyes off the monitor and turned to him.

"A heist?" He laughed again. "Perhaps. I mean

Viktoria and her father have plenty of money to buy art. They don't need to steal it or hire someone to steal it for them. However, money isn't always the issue. Some of these collectors want specific works for their private collections. Famous pieces that aren't for sale and never will be. They'll go to great lengths to acquire them."

"So you think that's what's happening here?" Just when I thought I couldn't sink any deeper into the intrigue, was I now neck deep in the international world of art smuggling?

Tristan shook his head. "No. The location doesn't seem right for it. There is obviously security on site—both guards and cameras—yet they don't seem concerned about it." Glancing at me, he cocked one brow high. "Speaking of guards . . . Perhaps we should watch for our friend so we're not the ones suspected of your heist."

The *we* in that sentence was me since watching for the return of the guard was my assignment and I was shirking it.

I moved back to my post by the door and listened for a second. No sound of voices or footsteps or elevator movement caught my attention. I leaned out and looked both ways, then leaned back in.

"Still clear." I announced, and then glanced at Tristan. "So we found her. What's next? Are we going to keep watch from here and see where she goes next or can we get out of here now?"

Tristan hit a few more keys on the console. "We can't stay here for long. I've got Alex and the guard still on the floor above us." He frowned and laughed. "She has him crawling on the floor."

"What? Why?" I asked.

"If I had to guess, she's pretending she was here during business hours and lost something precious, jewelry most likely. She's convinced him to help her look for it. That's what I would do." Tristan spoke as his fingers flew over the keyboard. "She's good. I'll give her that."

He glanced up at me and chuckled.

I could only assume he noticed that his compliment of Alex's powers of deception had brought the scowl back to my face.

"Don't blame her, Hearst. We all have done regrettable things for the job." He stood and moved away from the monitors.

"Not me," I returned, feeling righteous.

"You've been working this assignment for how long?" he asked.

"About a week." I shrugged.

He shook his head. "For her—and for me—it's not a passing diversion. It's our lives. That makes a difference."

I considered his words but held onto my anger. "Then you both should choose a different life."

To my surprise, Tristan laughed. "That's very possibly true." He moved to stand next to me in the doorway. "Time to go."

"Where?"

"To find out what our lovely heiress is up to."

"What about Alex?" I asked. Not that I cared but it seemed lax to leave a member of the team behind.

"We'll catch up with her back at the party."

"Did you tell her that?" I asked, keeping my voice low as we made our way down the hallway.

"No." He stopped, leaned around the corner, then proceeded full steam ahead.

As I rushed to keep up, I asked, "Then how can you be sure she'll know to meet us back there?"

"Because it's what I would do."

I was beginning to see a pattern here. Apparently all spies—both good guys and bad guys—drew from the same playbook. One that I, as a spectator, had never been privy to.

He was right. It was a different world. A different life.

Even if I could justify her actions and forgive Alex—even if it turned out she was working for the good side—we operated in completely different worlds with a different set of rules.

Back when I thought she was a struggling college student I'd assumed the challenge for us would arise from her not being able to relate to my life as a Hearst.

Little did I know the hurdle between us wouldn't be my being rich, but instead her being a spy.

I was just considering how fucking insane that was when Tristan body slammed me into a dark doorway and pressed a finger to his lips to tell me to be silent.

The elevator shaft rumbled as the car neared our floor, then there was the distinct sound of the doors swooshing open.

My heart pounded, so hard and fast I actually feared the guard would hear it.

He didn't of course. He moved past, en route to the post he'd abandoned prior to Alex stumbling into his life. He'd gotten away easy as far as I was concerned. She's caused a lot more damage when she'd stumbled into mine.

Finally, Tristan motioned for me to follow him.

I glanced down the hall before rushing after Tristan.

We stopped in front of the elevator. As the doors opened once again a realization hit me.

I somehow managed to control my outburst until they'd slid shut. Then I spun to Tristan. "The guard's going to see us on the monitors. And Victoria too."

Tristan shook his head. "No, he won't."

"But—"

"I put the cameras on a loop showing this elevator, the storage room and the hallway leading to it as empty."

I sagged against the wall of the elevator and let out a breath. "Okay."

Tristan punched a button and glanced back at me. "You all right, mate?"

The answer to that was a resounding no, but I wasn't going to admit that to James Bond here, so instead I said, "Yeah. All good."

He smiled. "You'll get used to it."

"I doubt that." And after today, I seriously hoped I wasn't in this life long enough to get accustomed to it because what I'd experienced of it so far was completely fucked up.

NINETEEN

The elevator rumbled into motion and I glanced at Tristan.

He looked cool and collected. Bored almost. Meanwhile, I was sweating in spite of the air conditioning.

Of the two of us, I had to think mine was the more rational reaction.

We were about to step out into the middle of God only knew what. We could possibly be interrupting a majorly illegal art deal.

I realized that didn't sound quite as ominous as interrupting a major drug deal but I figured it could be dangerous nonetheless. We were talking high dollar stolen goods here. Some pieces went for millions of dollars at auction. I could only imagine a thief wouldn't be happy to be interrupted.

I missed having Zane in my ear to calm me down. Even him calling me Rosebud would have helped at the moment.

Instead, the only person I had to lean on was mister cool here and he didn't look like the coddling type.

All too soon the elevator came to a stop and the doors opened.

I reached my hand into my pocket where I'd stashed Alex's gun. I wasn't so sure it was a good idea to whip it out and threaten the possible art thieves with it, but it made me feel better knowing it was an option should it become necessary.

I struggled to get the gun out of my pocket, which was cut way too small for this. I wondered if Tristan had his suits custom made specifically to accommodate his weapons. I probably should have been paying more attention to not shooting myself in the foot instead as I struggled to get the weapon free.

Next to me Tristan stiffened and my focus whipped to him.

"What?" I asked, as softly as I could in spite of my panic.

He mouthed for me to shush and then I saw his weapon was out.

Jesus. What was happening? I didn't know but I needed to be prepared for it. If I could only get the damn gun out—

"About time you two got here." Alex's voice drew my attention away from the struggle in my pocket.

"Fancy seeing you here." Tristan visibly relaxed and took a step out of the elevator car.

"Viktoria is in the storage room at the end of the hall," Alex informed Tristan with barely a glance in my direction.

Yup, the honeymoon was over. She wasn't even pretending to care what I thought anymore.

No more honey pot for me. I sucked it up and focused on the situation. There'd be time for wallowing and anger later.

"How did you know she was here?" I asked Alex.

"The guard got a call on his radio while I was with him. One of the other guys telling him a major donor and her guest were getting a private tour from the curator of the collection not on view."

"We believe that?" I asked Tristan. I'd love for him to say everything was fine and we could go back to the party and get a drink.

"I guess we'll find out," he said.

My eyes widened at the implications of that. "What are we going to do? Confront her?"

"I am. You're not." Tristan shot me a look.

"What do you mean?" I sure as hell didn't want to go into that storeroom but I didn't want to be left behind either.

"You're staying here," Tristan informed me.

"I think I should go in. Alone," Alex said.

"Thanks, love, but I don't think so."

I was happy to see Tristan didn't trust her either. At least we were on the same page as far as that went.

Alex scowled. "Fine. We go in together."

Tristan hesitated, looking as if he was considering Alex's suggestion. He finally nodded. "All right. We go in pretending to be a drunk couple who snuck away from the party looking for a place to get amorous."

She nodded as I frowned, not sure I liked that plan. But it was too late. With barely a backward glance, they were gone, leaving me behind as they moved down the hall toward the storage room.

If I were honest with myself, I'd admit I was pouting not only about being left behind, but also about the fact the smooth Brit was about to get handsy with the woman I'd considered my girl for a couple of glorious, delusional days.

Even if it was a lie on her part, it hadn't been on mine and I really didn't like the idea of him touching her. Kissing her. Even pretending to be with her.

I jumped as the sound of the elevator moving broke into my self pity.

I tried to calm myself by reviewing the many reasons why that elevator was in use. There was still a party happening on the fifth floor. Guests arriving late, other guests leaving early. Any number of them could have called for the elevator rather than take the escalator up and down all those flights.

It was a perfectly reasonable explanation . . . until I watched the numbers above the elevator change, creeping closer and closer to the floor I was standing on, and then stop.

Holy shit.

Those doors were going to open and I was standing right there in front of them in full view of whoever was inside.

Maybe the guard had come to check on Viktoria.

It didn't matter who it was, I didn't want to be seen here where I didn't belong. I didn't trust myself to be able to pull off a ruse like Tristan and Alex were—pretending to be drunk and lost or whatever. It was safer to just stay out of sight.

Luckily for me this floor, like the other one we'd been on, wasn't lacking in doorways.

I spun and held my breath while I turned the doorknob, hoping it wasn't locked.

It opened and I slipped into the darkened office, leaving the door open just a crack so I could peer out.

I didn't have to see the two men to be concerned because I heard them speaking to one another—and they were speaking in Russian. But what I did see from my hiding spot had my breath catching in my throat.

The pair of men had guns and they were already out.

I fumbled with my cell and punched in a text to Zane in all caps.

WARN TRISTAN! 2 ARMED RUSSIANS HEADING HIS WAY.

I cursed Alex one more time for taking my best means of communication with Zane from me when she smashed my comm, but at least I still had the cell . . . and I had her gun.

My eyes widened when I remembered that.

Should I follow the men? It was two against one but I did have the element of surprise on my side. Although they would too if Zane hadn't gotten the text and warned Tristan.

I glanced at the cell and saw no reply. That could be because he was busy talking to Tristan. Or it could be because he hadn't checked his phone.

I had to follow up.

DO YOU COPY?!

Thank God for autocorrect—that was a sentence I never thought I'd ever say or even think. But with the adrenaline making my hands shake, I butchered the text and somehow the program fixed it for me and correctly—proof miracles did happen.

Zane's reply lit up my screen sending a glow throughout the dark room.

Copy

I blew out a breath. At least he'd get word to Tristan and Alex, but would it be in time? How long was this hallway anyway? How far away was the storage room?

I didn't know the answer.

Leaning into the hall I strained to hear any sound. If I heard gunshots I was going in. It didn't matter if I didn't know Viktoria, barely knew Tristan and didn't trust Alex, I couldn't leave them alone and not try to help if the shit hit the fan.

The museum guards wouldn't even know if anything happened because Tristan had looped the monitors for this wing. I supposed I could call for the guards. Or even 9-1-1.

Explaining the situation to the cops would be interesting but we could deal with that issue later— once we were all safe and alive.

A loud noise from down the hall made me jump. What was it?

It was too far away to tell. Had it been a gunshot or something else?

Shaking harder than before I typed in a text to Zane.

I HEARD SOMETHING! GUNSHOT?

It felt like an eternity until his reply came back, although I'm sure it was mere seconds.

Stay put.

Stay put. Easy for him to say.

My mind raced. One noise. Possibly one gunshot. There were two unidentified armed Russian men, three people total in that clandestine meeting of Viktoria's, and then Tristan and Alex.

So the question remained, if that had been a gunshot, from whose gun did it originate and, more importantly, who had been the target?

TWENTY

I remained frozen with indecision when the sound of male voices had me backing into my hiding place once again.

Russian words caught my ear and I vowed to learn the damn language if I got out of here alive.

The men passed my position and headed to the elevator.

They stood, nonchalantly waiting for it to come, as if they hadn't just possibly left a body bleeding out behind them.

One began speaking. I couldn't see, but since it was a one sided conversation I assumed he was talking on a comm or cell phone. I seriously hoped he wasn't reporting to his superior the successful elimination of whoever their target was.

That I didn't hear anything else was extremely odd. No screams. No sirens. No voices at all except for the two Russians by the elevator.

I was deciding if that was comforting or

disturbing when the elevator opened and the men stepped inside.

The doors slid shut and the sound of the voices faded.

That was it. I'd had enough of hiding and staying put. I needed to find out what had happened.

I popped my head out of the doorway. With a glance at the elevator to make sure the coast was clear I took off down the hall toward where I'd heard the sound.

My hope was to find the rest of my team—upright and breathing.

Dress shoes were not made for running, but I made progress, sprinting past closed doors that looked more office than storage until I reached the end of the hall.

There I skidded to a stop at what I saw. The doorknob was mangled, as if someone had shot the lock.

That explained the sound I'd heard but didn't answer the more pressing question—where was everyone?

I should call or text Zane. I could also head back to the party and wait for Tristan and Alex to come out of hiding. I did neither.

Instead I pushed open the door and stepped inside.

Silence greeted me. I decided I'd had enough of the silence and enough of being in the dark, both figuratively and literally. I flipped on the lights.

"Tristan!" I had no patience as I waited for a reply. "Alex? Viktoria? Dammit, someone answer me!"

"You need to learn to do as you're told." Tristan stepped out of the shadows. The cocky crooked grin on his face was such a relief I couldn't even be angry at his words.

"Thank God." A breath whooshed out of me. "I heard a shot. I was worried. Is everyone okay?"

As I looked around the space I heard more voices speaking Russian, but this time they were female.

Viktoria. And Alex? I saw them now through the open shelving of the storeroom.

It shouldn't be a surprise Alex spoke Russian. Nothing that woman did could surprise me anymore. Though the overwhelming relief that she was all right shocked the hell out of me.

Maybe I did have it in me to forgive her— eventually.

Tristan stepped closer and glanced at the doorway. "Russians shot the lock. They gone?" he asked.

"Yes," I answered, hoping it was the truth. "I waited until they got on the elevator then came to investigate. Who were they?"

Tristan shrugged. "Could be anyone. NSB. Putin's henchmen. Viktoria's daddy's men. Who knows?"

"Jesus." That list of possibilities, here on US soil and at the MoMA no less, did not make me feel better.

Tristan's gaze met mine. "Thanks for the warning. You saved us from quite a mess. We were able to hide before they got here."

So that's what had happened. The Russians found an empty room and thought their target had left. But that didn't explain what was happening here in the first place.

"Care to explain what's going on there?" I tipped my head toward Viktoria, the two men who looked as pale and shaken as I felt, and Alex who seemed perfectly calm in spite of it all.

Tristan followed my gaze. "Apparently Alex speaks fluent Russian."

I cocked up a brow. "Yes, I see that. But what was Viktoria doing creeping around here in the first place, and why were two armed men tailing her? Did we stumble upon some sort of smuggling ring?"

It was quite obvious that this wasn't just a donor taking a tour of the collection, even to me, a novice at this spy stuff.

"Actually, we did in a way. However, she's not smuggling art, but rather artists."

My gaze shot to him. "What?"

"My Russian isn't quite as good as Alex's—which is quite flawless by the way—but from what I've gathered, Viktoria is helping that man flee his country." Tristan nodded toward the man standing between Viktoria and Alex.

So many revelations came from that sentence I didn't know which to focus on first. That Alex's Russian was perfect—and what did that indicate about her? That Tristan also spoke Russian—of course he did. Why not? The man could do anything apparently. And finally—and this was probably the only thing I should be concerned about—that Viktoria was helping some artist defect.

"Why is he fleeing his country?" I asked, putting aside my petty personal concerns about Alex's identity and Tristan's perfection and settling on that last larger point.

"The subject of his art, and I'd wager his political leanings as well, has put him on Putin's hit list. Viktoria got him into the country on her private plane. The museum curator is helping set him up with a place to live and work here in the States."

I frowned. "I didn't know being an artist was such a dangerous profession."

"Under certain countries, it definitely is."

It was like the plot of an action movie. I was still trying to wrap my head around it all when I asked Tristan, "What now?"

"Now you can go back to the party or home if you wish. We're done here."

"Done?" It didn't feel done. The bad guys could still be in the building. Viktoria's artist was still stashed in the storeroom of the museum. It felt like there were too many loose ends for this to be over. "What about him?"

"There's a car waiting at the loading dock to take the artist away."

"But what if the two Russians are down there waiting for him?"

"Zane's computer expert has gained access to a camera across the street. He's got eyes on the car and the surrounding area. It's clear, but I'm going down with them to make sure."

"So you don't need me?" I asked.

"No. We're good, mate. Go get yourself a drink. You deserve it."

"Okay." Why was I feeling so let down?

Maybe because if this had been an action movie,

there'd be some sort of conclusion. A happy ending. At least a kiss before the hero left his lady and drove off into the sunset.

Yeah, that wasn't going to happen.

I glanced at Alex, still chatting in Russian, and then back to Tristan. "I think I'll skip that drink and just head out."

And then have a drink—or three—once I was safely home, alone in my apartment.

I had a feeling I was going to need it.

TWENTY-ONE

The day ended completely differently than it had started.

I'd left for the museum happy with Alex in my passenger seat. I'd driven home alone and depressed.

The malaise followed me all the way back to Jersey where I unlocked the door of my apartment. The place I'd spent twenty-four hours getting to know Alex.

Now I knew I hadn't known her at all.

The wet towels from our showers were gone. Washed and folded and put away. The bed, the scene of so much of my recent time with her, was made. The sheets were probably freshly washed as well, knowing my overachieving housekeeper who'd come to clean, expecting me to be in Virginia by now.

But none of that erased the memories . . . or the anger. Or the underlying ache that bordered on pain colored with disappointment.

I'd lived alone my whole life and never minded it. Enjoyed it actually, but for the first time my home felt lonely.

At a loss for what to do with myself, I moved to the kitchen and stood in front of the open refrigerator door. I'd never gotten around to eating anything at the event and it was well past dinnertime now. I should be hungry, but I wasn't really. This felt more like restlessness not hunger.

When the doorbell rang I closed the fridge and moved toward the door. I reached for the knob and then hesitated.

I'd gotten a good look at the more sinister side of life recently. The world of spies and defectors. I'd been up close and personal with good guys and bad and those who operated in that gray space in between.

For the first time ever I considered who might be on the other side of the door and if it was safe to open it.

It didn't matter if the building was secure. The museum was supposedly secure too and I'd watched the guards be misdirected and deceived easily by both Alex and Tristan and their various skills.

Blowing out a breath I chided myself for even worrying. My days as ad hoc spy were over. My world consisted of board meetings and emptying my inbox once again. No one was coming to my apartment to get me.

I should be so lucky to have that kind of excitement in my life—and I should be institutionalized for that last thought because a man in his right mind wouldn't wish for that kind of excitement, no matter how mundane his life felt without it.

Without further consideration, I yanked open my door and drew back at who stood there.

"Alex." My powers of scintillating conversation seemed to have gone out the window and that was the best I could come up with.

"Brent."

Against my will my pulse raced just at the sight of her at my door. "Why are you here?"

"You've got my gun." Her answer was matter of fact. The look in her eyes was anything but.

If I trusted my instincts I'd say she was as affected emotionally by our meeting as I was.

Unfortunately, I had proof I couldn't trust my instincts so I dismissed that idea . . . or at least tried to. The shadow of it remained because I wanted her to be hurting too. I liked the idea that she, like me, had gotten attached only to feel the pain of suddenly being unattached again.

"If I give it back to you, are you going to shoot me?" I asked. Sadly, it was a serious question.

I should probably take the bullets out before returning the weapon to her. It would give me a few seconds head start. Me against a trained operator—I figured I could use any advantage I could get.

"No." Her gaze dropped away. "Can I come in?"

When she brought her eyes back up to mine, I had a memory of the shy version of Alex I'd gotten to know first.

Then I remembered that had also been the fake, lying, manipulative honey pot Alex grooming me.

I moved back and she took the few steps forward that brought her inside my apartment. I closed the door, telling myself I'd only let her in because this wasn't a conversation I wanted the neighbors to hear.

It was probably better if they didn't see me handing over a gun in the hallway either.

It took me a second to locate the jacket I tossed on the back of the sofa when I'd arrived home. The gun in the pocket made it hang low over the side.

I reached inside and extracted the weapon from the fabric and then went the extra step to pop out the clip and check the chamber for a bullet like Zane had drilled into my head during our hour at the range. Hey, I pay attention sometimes.

I pocketed the clip and handed the gun to her, watching her react in response.

When she didn't turn to leave, but seemed to be waiting for something, I said, "You're not getting the ammunition so . . ."

She raised her gaze to meet mine. "Can we talk?"

I let out a sigh, feeling the weight of the past few days hit me.

"Why?" A lot had happened in a short amount of time and now that it was over, I wanted it to be just that—over. Talking wouldn't change or help anything. "What do you want from me, Alex?"

She laid down the gun on the table next to my keys.

Somehow, after all I'd been through today, the juxtaposition of those two items on my table didn't look as odd as it should.

"It wasn't—"

"It wasn't what, Alex? All a lie? I wasn't a job?" I was getting nice and mad, ramping up for a good fight when Alex took a step forward.

"Shut up." Her lips crashed against mine as she attacked me, pressing me back with the force of all that lean muscle I'd admired.

I expected her to attack me. I didn't expect her to kiss me.

And crap, I kissed her back.

There was nothing loving about it. It wasn't a healing kiss. It was hard and angry and God how I needed it.

Tangling her hair in my fist, I yanked her head back and thrust my tongue against hers. I backed her up until she smashed against the wall. I broke the kiss long enough to utter a curse. At her. At myself.

I hated her for lying to me but I still wanted her. For that I hated myself.

None of it mattered anyway. My desire was like an out of control freight train. There was no stopping it now.

Shoving all of my many emotions aside, I knew I was going to do it. I was going to fuck her.

And that's exactly what it would be. Fucking. This wasn't going to be making love. Nope. It was much too late for that. We were well past that.

She'd started this thing. I think I could have controlled myself if she hadn't. But now that she had, there was no stopping it.

"Take off your pants." My order came out sounding as angry as I felt.

She did, her deft fingers conquering the button and zipper quickly.

I was hard as a rock as I freed myself from my own pants. I shoved her face first against the back of the sofa, bending her at the waist.

Stepping up behind her, I took what I wanted, hard and fast.

I wasn't a small man—one girl I'd hooked up with in college had spread the rumor that my bank account wasn't the only big thing about me—but I didn't care that I might be hurting Alex now.

With one palm flat on her back, I braced myself with the other hand on her hip. I wasn't aware of much more than that except for the need to pound away my frustration.

I plunged inside her and tried to purge my own pain.

As I'd come to expect from Alex—at least this new version of her I'd gotten to know today—she gave as good as she got, thrusting back against me with a force that was nearly violent.

Her cries rose to a crescendo as I crashed into her until I felt myself on the brink.

Sanity returned just in the nick of time. I pulled out, coming on her back and hating myself for forgoing protection with a woman who was a proven liar.

Now I could resent her for making me lose my mind, in addition to everything else she'd done.

Why not? Someone had to share this blame I was piling on myself. After her deception she deserved more than a good dose of it.

I ran my hand over my face, trying to reconcile

what had just happened.

Apparently I couldn't resist her. That was on me. But whatever had brought her to my door and had her making the first move on me was on *her* . . . and so was quite a mess. All over her.

That part was my fault.

"Stay here. Don't move." Lips compressed with my bitter unhappiness, I yanked my briefs up, fastened my pants and strode to the kitchen to get a paper towel.

Back at the sofa where she was still bent temptingly, I stoically ignored the shape of her naked ass thrust in the air and wiped the worst of the mess off her skin.

Deciding that was good enough, I tossed the towels into the trash and folded my arms, keeping my distance by leaning against the end of the kitchen island.

"Why are you here, Alex?"

She glanced up at me as she pulled her underwear up. "I told you. I came to get my gun."

"Nothing else? You sure?" One possible reason why she might have pushed us back into a physical relationship struck me—obviously about ten minutes too late but hey, better late than never. "My computer is right over there. Feel free to hack into it when I go to the bathroom. But I'm warning you there's not much on there except work. Or are you here for my cell phone maybe? There's nothing much in there either but go for it. I'll even unlock it for you."

"I don't want to go through your computer or your phone."

I didn't believe her. Shaking my head at myself for even allowing the conversation to go this far I pushed off the counter.

"Get your gun and go. I'm taking a shower." I walked across the room toward the hallway. Without looking back, I said, "I expect you gone by the time I get out."

I headed into the bathroom intent on washing away the memories. Of her and of my own weakness. I knew what she was—a liar and a spy—and I'd given in anyway.

Yup, I could try to blame her but this one—this one was on me.

TWENTY-TWO

I was trying—and failing—to get some work done on the train to Virginia when my cell phone vibrated. I'd forgotten to set it to totally silent.

No surprise. My mind wasn't where it should be.

Grateful for the interruption since I couldn't concentrate anyway, I pulled it out of my pocket.

Zane's name appeared on the text.

You in town?

I scowled, remembering the last time he'd said that and summoned me to his office. That was how this whole mess had begun. Had it really only been two weeks ago?

Not bowing to his summons so easily this time, I typed in a question of my own.

Why?

I bet he really wouldn't like not getting an answer from me. I could picture his frown. Imagining his displeasure made me feel better.

Need to see you.

I couldn't really say no. I had the guy's gun and I certainly didn't want to keep it.

Even locked in the portable gun safe he'd loaned me along with the weapon I didn't like having it in the apartment or on the train.

I guess I wasn't like Zane. Or Tristan. Or Alex for that matter—comfortable wielding a weapon.

Resigned Zane was going to get his way if I wanted to rid myself of this gun locked in the box in my briefcase, making it twice as heavy as normal, I typed in a reply.

On the train now. Give me an hour.

The reply came back immediately.

Make it two hours.

What the hell? Now he was going to dictate when I complied with his summons? Although, it would do me no good to go over to the office early if he wouldn't be there.

I drew in a breath and gave in. This little visit was really going to put a dent in my workday productivity but I couldn't concentrate anyway.

Scowling, I responded.

Fine.

Even the idea of teasing Zane about his off-limits office manager Chelsea didn't brighten my mood. Alex had ruined me. Stolen my joy. And it was because of Zane I'd met Alex in the first place.

Happy my blame had come full circle, I gave up on work and settled in to wallow for the final few moments of my trip . . . and try not to remember my final moments with Alex.

I'd told her to be gone by the time I got out of

the shower and she had been.

For once the damn woman had done exactly as I asked. Didn't that figure?

I walked from the Amtrak station to my apartment to drop off my briefcase and laptop, figuring after the visit with Zane I might or might not be in the mood to head to the office. I was betting on *not*.

By the time I got settled in, made a phone call to the office in New Jersey and another to the office in Virginia, it was time for me to leave for Zane's.

Grabbing the gun safe, I transferred it into a duffle bag and headed out again to the station, this time to hop on the Metro to Dupont Circle. That wasn't too nerve wracking, riding the Metro with a damn gun in my bag.

Was transporting it this close to the Capitol even legal? I didn't know but by the time I stepped from the street and into Zane's door I was good and agitated.

Lucky for me he was standing in the outer office so I didn't have to wait to bitch to him.

"Here's your damn gun back." I tossed the duffle bag onto the chair in front of me. "And next time—"

I didn't have a chance to tell him about next time because Alex stepped out of Zane's office.

"I believe you two know each other." The bastard had the nerve to act as if he didn't know exactly how well I knew Alex.

Fine. I could act too. I pretended my heart wasn't thundering just from the sight of her.

"Alex." I delivered a cool nod in her direction and then looked at my friend. "Zane, a word?"

"Of course." He turned toward his office, addressing Alex as he said, "Give us a moment?"

"Sure."

Just my walking past her in the narrow space seemed a feat. To celebrate my accomplishment, I closed the door nice and hard, between us.

Even with the door shut, I didn't feel confident she wouldn't hear everything I said.

On second thought, good. Let her hear. She deserved to know how I felt about her now.

"What's she doing here?" I asked.

"Interviewing for a position."

"With you? You're hiring her?"

"Like it or not, she's good."

"She's a liar."

"She's an undercover operator. There's a difference."

"I don't see one."

"Because you're mad and behaving like a brat."

I frowned. "Fuck you."

For once, Zane didn't laugh at me when I got frustrated and cursed at him. Instead he actually looked sincere. Almost concerned.

It was confusing. I didn't know what to do with the reaction.

"Brent, she wants to talk. To explain. I think you should listen to her."

I shook my head. "So you two are all chummy now, talking about your mutual friend Brent? I thought she was here to interview."

"She is, and her past job performance is a critical piece of information. And you are part of that."

"I don't like it. I don't trust her. Do you even know who or what she is? Tristan said she spoke Russian like a native. Did you ever wonder why? Huh? I think she's KGB or NSB or whatever the fuck they're called now. Probably sent here to set up a sleeper cell."

"That's a TV show."

"It also happens in real life," I defended.

"I need you to trust me. Do you?" Zane asked.

I didn't want to admit it but finally I did. "Yes . . . Mostly."

One brow rose at my last minute qualifier, but he didn't comment on it. "Then trust that I had her checked out with every resource at my disposal. Plus some."

"And?" I asked, curious in spite of myself.

"She definitely has a colorful background, and her being raised by Russian-speaking parents is part of that, but we found no red flags."

"Not even her association with Blackwater?"

"I might not agree with their methods but they're a legitimate company." He lifted a shoulder. "Look, just listen to what she has to say. You can decide for yourself what to think after you hear her out. That's all I'm asking."

I drew in a breath and let it out in a burst. "Fine."

"Good." Zane stood and moved toward the door, pausing by where I still stood. "Try to keep an open mind. Okay?"

"Why?" I asked.

"Because I think you really care about this girl."

I let out a snort. "That's not a good thing."

"It is if she cares about you too." Zane the philosopher cocked a brow as if daring me to consider that and then opened the door.

He left and Alex appeared in the open doorway.

I shook my head at the ridiculousness of this. "Come on in. Might as well shut the door too, although Zane probably has the place bugged."

"I do not." The muffled denial came through the door as Alex clicked it closed.

She turned to me looking less like a Russian-speaking, gun and shoe-wielding bad-ass and more like the student volunteer I'd first met.

She raised that enticing emerald gaze to meet mine. "I'm sorry."

I let out a short laugh. "Me too."

Sorry I'd let myself fall too hard too fast.

A one-night stand I could have bounced back from. This was proving much harder.

"I want to tell you everything."

"Look, Alex . . ." I was going to tell her it didn't even matter anymore when a thought stopped me mid-sentence and I asked, "Is Alex even your real name?"

"Alexandra Svetlana Petrushev. But I really do go by Alex." Before I could stop her she continued, "I was born in Russia but my parents moved us to the States when I was three. We only spoke Russian at home. That's why I speak it."

"So you're not KGB, or NSB, or whatever?"

"I'm not."

"Why were you in the Hamptons?" I asked, obviously interested even though I really did not want to be.

"I was told to be there, because Viktoria was there."

"Why?"

"I don't know. I was just a foot soldier. We didn't know the whys. Just told what to do and we did it."

"And what were you told to do?"

"I was to observe and report back everything I saw. When I told them I suspected you were there for other reasons than the fundraiser, they told me to find out more.

"So you slept with me." Those words tasted bitter in my mouth.

"No."

When I cocked up a brow, challenging her answer, she sighed.

"Yes, I slept with you, but they never told me to or expected me to spend the night with you."

"Going above and beyond the call of duty to get information out of me, were you?" I spat. "Bet that's the kind of dedication that gets you a promotion."

"I wasn't using sex to get information out of you."

"Then why did you come back to my place?"

"Because I wanted to. I was attracted to you."

My doubt must have shown on my face.

She continued, "And yes, I was looking for more information. But I didn't need to sleep with you to get all that information. I'd already put a tracker on your car at the Hamptons party. That's how I followed you to the donut shop in Montauk."

I turned away from her, feeling ill. I'd been holding on to our shared love of those damn jelly croissants as the last genuine memory I had of her. Now that was spoiled as well.

Shaking my head, I spun back to glare at her. "I should have realized the Bake Shop was a lie too. You probably never even heard of the place."

"No. Not true."

"Don't." I held up a hand to stop her from piling more lies on the already overwhelmingly high pile.

"No, Brent. Listen to me. I grew up in Brighton Beach. My parents used to take my sister and me to Montauk every summer. We'd rent one of those tiny rooms with bunk beds in the hotel over by the docks and watch the fishermen come in every evening. And every morning, we'd go to town for jelly sticks." She pressed her right hand over her heart. "I swear to you on my grandmother's memory."

"Well, at least that was real."

"It was all real. I cared about you. I wanted to prove to myself you were innocent. But the evidence kept piling up. The comm in your car. Your connection to Zane. How you reacted every time I mentioned Viktoria. And I hated every new thing that made me suspect you were at that party spying on her."

"Spying on her. Like you were." I conveniently left out how I was there to spy on Viktoria's comrade Alexey.

She shrugged. "It was work."

While we were on the topic of Viktoria and Alex was supposedly being so forthcoming, I asked, "Tell me what was happening in the storeroom at the museum. What was Viktoria up to?"

"She flew an artist from Russia here in her jet. Her father's jet actually."

"Why?" I asked.

"More and more Russian artists are defying Putin. Crackdowns on freedom of speech are driving them into exile. Some of the more subversive artists have already fled to Berlin."

I had done my homework recently, studying Viktoria and her family in Russia. I knew what she had done would not go over well if exposed, considering how close her father was with Putin. Maybe that was why Alex had been put on her trail.

"Did you report all this to your boss?"

She shook her head. "No."

I cocked up a brow. "Really. Why not? This sounds like something they'd be interested in."

"I'm sure they would have been very interested but I decided to do what I felt was right. And then I resigned."

Which is why she was here looking for a job with Zane. I should probably get a finder's fee for this. She'd likely have never heard his name if it hadn't been for me.

"When Zane called, the timing was perfect."

I frowned. "Wait. Zane called you?"

She nodded. "He said he liked the way I handled

the situation at the museum."

"You crushed his communicator with your shoe." That was destruction of property. And I didn't even know how much the damn thing cost to replace.

She shrugged. "It had a tracker in it. He said he would have done the same thing."

I doubted I'd ever get the hang of this spy stuff and after this past week, I was fine with that. But that still left this thing with us up in the air.

"I do mean it. I'm sorry for every lie I told you. Every time I doubted you. And every second I hurt you."

"You didn't hurt me." Now I was lying.

"Good, I'm glad. Because I sure hurt the hell out of myself coming to your place. I shouldn't have. I've never felt such pain as when you told me to leave right after . . ." She cleared her throat and didn't finish the sentence, not that I could have forgotten what we'd done. "Anyway, I understand. I mean I lied. You're mad. You have every right to be—"

"Stop talking." I hauled her against me, kissing her before the whirlwind that was my emotions had me saying something I might regret later.

I kissed her hard, and held her harder, like she was a buoy and I was a drowning man.

Hell, I was drowning. In her kiss. In my feelings.

Sinking into her felt good. Probably too good considering all that had happened between us, but I didn't fight it.

When I pulled back, out of necessity so we could

both take a much needed breath, I saw the concern and emotion in her eyes. I was pretty unsteady in that area myself.

"Does this mean you forgive me?" she asked.

I thought about that, considering the question before I answered.

What had she done that I hadn't done myself?

She'd lied. I'd lied. We'd both had to in the course of our crazy assignments.

She'd been there to keep an eye on Viktoria. She wasn't sure exactly why. I'd been there to keep an eye on Alexey for Zane's unnamed client while I wasn't exactly sure why either.

If she spoke the truth, she'd spent that first night with me because of an attraction she couldn't fight in spite of not knowing if she could trust me or not. I'd taken her in my apartment two nights ago under the same circumstances.

Remembering her angry sex face that first time, it seemed we both hated ourselves for our weakness, yet it didn't stop either of us. We'd done it anyway.

The way I saw it now, we were pretty much even in all of the bullshit that had happened between us.

The only difference was that I was ready to end all the intrigue, while she was applying for a job that would ensure it continued.

It had been a week filled with deception for me and already I'd had enough. It was exhausting. I couldn't even imagine how Alex felt after making a career of it.

Zane too. This is how he'd spent his years in the

SEALs after we'd left school—except with the added challenge of traveling to places where the enemy would try to kill him.

How the hell did someone carry on a normal existence after a decade of that? I felt changed after just a week of it.

I had new respect for him. For everyone in this line of work. Publishing might be boring in comparison but I'd take it.

And speaking of my boring life, the time had come to decide what was next for us.

I drew in a breath. "There's nothing to forgive."

As she looked visibly relieved, I leaned down to press my forehead against hers.

"What now?" I asked.

I mean, I could think of plenty of things to do in the immediate future, bringing her back to my apartment and making up for that last incredibly strange time we'd been together being top of the list, but what about after that?

What about the future? Did we have one given how different our lives were? Did she even want one with me?

She raised her gaze to meet mine hesitantly. "If Zane hires me, I'll have a new job. I'd be based out of New York with a lot of trips down here. Maybe we could see each other, since I'll be nearby."

I forced the excitement down. I was determined to take things slower with her this time, but I couldn't help but be uplifted that the two places Alex mentioned happened to be conveniently close to where I spent most of my time.

"He'll hire you," I said. He would if I had anything to do about it. After this week I figured Zane now owed me. "And yeah. We can see each other. I'd like that."

The tiniest of smiles bowed her lips. "Me too."

EPILOGUE

Eyes locked, muscles tensed, we squared off. On alert. Ready. Each waiting for the other to make the first move.

"Come on. Come at me." I urged her forward with a small wave of my raised hands.

She shook her head. "Why don't you come at me?"

"All right." Without pause, I pounced, taking her off guard and off her feet with one swift move.

We ended up with her, flat on her back and me above her. Just as I liked it.

I smiled. "I win."

I'd learned some things over the past few months. Enough I could now take Alex when we sparred. Not as often as she bested me, but I was working on it.

"I let you win," she said.

"Bull shit." I frowned and tried to decide if she was lying to me or not.

She smiled and fisted my T-shirt in one hand, yanking me forward and down until I was just a breath from her face. "Kiss me."

"Not until you tell me the truth." I locked my elbows and remained just out of reach of her lips. "Did you let me win?"

"No." The way she screwed up her pretty mouth as she answered told me it was indeed the truth, and she wasn't happy about it.

That made me happy.

Trying to control my triumphant grin and be a good sport, I leaned in. Her honesty deserved a reward. A kiss for now, and a much bigger reward later when we were in private.

"Thank you." I bracketed her head with my forearms and kissed her, hard and thorough. Probably inappropriate for the gym in my Alexandria apartment building but fuck it. We were alone, for the moment, and I paid enough in rent I should be able to do whatever I wanted on the exercise mats—including giving Alex that big reward.

Hmm, would she go for that? It might be fun . . .

Before I could consider further, I found myself on my back with Alex over me, smiling. "Ha!"

I laughed. "That doesn't count."

"It always counts." She leaned low and took control of the kiss and I couldn't really complain about the sudden reversal in our positions.

With my hands on her hips I pressed her against my very happy length, growing harder by the second, and decided that maybe I should be letting her win instead of trying to beat her if this was the result.

I was about to suggest we get naughty next to the Nautilus machine when the clearing of a throat drew my attention.

I tipped my head way back and peered behind me to see who Alex was looking at and who had disturbed my bliss.

"Zane," I said.

"Rosebud," he replied with a smile.

Alex giggled. He'd already filled her in on the whole story. Now they both enjoyed teasing me.

"Dickhead." I rolled my eyes. "I'm going to tell the doorman to stop letting you in."

"You can try but he works for me occasionally and since I'm sure GAPS pays him better than the management of this place, I'm pretty sure his loyalty lies with me."

That figured. I should have realized the guy at the front door looked a little too military for his job title.

I sighed. The more I hung out with Zane and Alex, the more I realized there were very few people who were actually who they seemed.

To add to my growing misery, Alex pushed off the mat and stood. "I'm going to shower. Meet you upstairs?" she asked.

"Will do." Maybe if I could ditch Zane quick, I could join her in that shower and finish what we started.

She grabbed her bottle of water and towel, nodded a goodbye to Zane and pushed through the glass door of the gym.

When she was gone and I'd finally gotten up off the floor myself, he cocked up one brow. "So, you two living together now?"

"No. Well not full-time anyway. Only when we're down here. She still has her apartment in Queens."

The one that I'd finally gotten inside. She hadn't kept me out of it because she had a roommate, which she didn't. She'd prevented me from coming inside because it was set up like a frigging spy lair. Assorted weapons of all types. Surveillance equipment. Photos pinned up on a corkboard. State of the art computers. Even body armor.

Zane nodded. "She ever actually sleep in that apartment in Queens?" he asked.

"Occasionally." I knew what he was getting at. We were as good as living together and it was too soon for that.

On a cerebral level, I agreed. But on a visceral level, I was more than ready to take things to the next level with Alex. And I had a feeling we would, soon.

I hadn't discussed it with her yet, but I knew her lease was up in the spring. Perfect timing for us to officially move in together.

"Comment?" I asked Zane.

If he didn't approve he might as well come right out with it now rather than beating around the bush.

"Not really." He shook his head.

"No?" I asked, shocked.

"Don't look so surprised. I like her." He lifted

one shoulder in a shrug.

I scowled. I wasn't used to Zane supporting my decisions. I didn't know what to think about it.

"So, the reason I came by . . ." he began.

Finally. I had been wondering the reason for his unannounced social call.

"Yes?"

"Any chance you've seen or heard from Chelsea today?"

"Your office manager? No." The only time I saw her was when I was at his office visiting him or Alex.

"Can you ask Alex for me, whenever you two are *done*."

I frowned. If he was really worried about Chelsea I could control my libido long enough to ask Alex if she'd heard from her.

In fact, I'd do it right now. I reached for where I'd left my cell phone and punched in a text.

As expected, Alex responded right away. She was addicted to her phone. She probably had it in the damn shower with her.

"She hasn't heard from her either." I tossed my cell back onto the table and reached for my water bottle. "Why? What's up?"

He hesitated.

Jesus, all we'd been through and he was still afraid to tell me things?

I clenched my jaw, about to tell him off when he said, "There's a chance she might be missing."

My eyes widened.

I'd had almost three solid months of no

excitement except for what Alex and I created between the sheets. But I supposed all good things came to an end.

As I waited for Zane to reveal the details in his own good time, all I could think was, *here we go again.*

Don't miss Chelsea and Tristan's stories in
Hot Chick for Hire
Spy for Hire

FOR HIRE
A Hot SEALs Series Spin-Off

Hot SEALs

For more titles by Cat visit CatJohnson.net

ABOUT THE AUTHOR

Cat Johnson is a top 10 *New York Times* bestseller and the author of the *USA Today* bestselling Hot SEALs series. She writes contemporary romance featuring sexy alpha heroes and is known for her unique marketing. She has sponsored pro bull riders, owns a collection of camouflage and western wear for book signings, and has used bologna to promote romance novels.

Never miss a new release or a deal again.
Join Cat's VIP Reader List at
catjohnson.net/news

Made in the USA
Las Vegas, NV
10 January 2025

16200141R00114